To

CW00692465

...ment

28.1.94

Fading Sounds and Discords

Fading Sounds & Discords

Michael A. Smith

The Book Guild Ltd.
Sussex, England

The Book Guild Ltd.
25 High Street,
Lewes, Sussex

First published 1994
© Michael A Smith 1994
Set in Baskerville
Typesetting by Acorn Bookwork,
Salisbury, Wiltshire
Printed in Great Britain by
Antony Rowe Ltd.
Chippenham, Wiltshire.

A catalogue record for this book is available from the British Library

ISBN 0 86332 903 9

To Anna, who has brought music into my life, and that is without her piano playing.

1

Jules Osk put the flannel to his face carefully, palpably. Then he squeezed it dry and placed it on the rim of the washbasin. It lay there, a misshapen lump. He swirled the soapy water with his hands and pulled out the plug.

The suds eddied round and disappeared down the plug-hole with a sudden surge followed by a cavernous gurgle which Jules did not hear, for he was going deaf.

This evening Jules was giving a piano recital at the Wigmore Hall, an honour to which he had aspired for much of his twenty-five years. His father Peter had booked a taxi from their home in recognition of the occasion and his mother Mary was gazing anxiously out of the front window against its arrival.

Jules came into the room and Mary turned towards him.

'Hurry up dear.' She unconsciously mouthed the words so that he should hear.

'I'm ready Mother.' He wiggled his fingers in the air and smiled at her.

Peter regarded him contentedly. He pondered the man Jules had become, his curly brown hair, slightly receding at the front, his rather prominent hazel eyes, so alert and expressive, the full lips and cheeks. He'll have to be careful, he thought, or he'll run to fat like Byron. There was a resemblance.

Mary saw the taxi draw up and opened her front door. Peter heard the quiet purring throb.

'Come on Jules. Mount your chariot. The honour's yours today.'

They rode together through suburban streets, cocooned in

that bond of unity which develops in a family over the years and locks them solid in times of stress or endeavour.

Peter was a phlegmatic fifty-eight-year-old and often wondered how he had sired such a sensitive offshoot as Jules. He was inclined to ascribe most of the artistic temperament in Jules to Mary, especially when the passions boiled over.

For some time Jules had suffered from a buzzing first in one ear and then in the other followed in due course by increasing deafness. Medical advice had been sought and found unable to offer any help of substance.

This evening the buzzing was severe, as tended to be the case when Jules was stressed, and his hearing correspondingly impaired. The affliction had served to intensify his endeavour to perfect his interpretation and technique on the piano and he sensed that tonight might well witness the peak of his achievements. This feeling of now or never had managed to beam its urgency across to his parents.

It was still quite light, with steel-grey undulant clouds riding high, with a hint of rose, as he glanced down Wigmore Street. Taxis purred by and the chunk of closing doors, like the muffled rattle of a spoon on the side of a bowl of cream, mingled with the chatter of other arrivals.

The three entered under the glass porch, supported by its slender black and gold columns, and bore down the long corridor which Jules had so often traversed as a student. This time it seemed different, but its familiar red carpet and cream walls with a dado of rose coloured marble reassured him. He was one of 'them' this time, one of the establishment, as it were. Part of the fittings, if only for tonight.

His parents were escorted to their seats in the front row and Jules noticed Boris Striman sitting at the side. He nodded over and Boris smiled back. They had known each other since childhood and the friendship had continued through their student days, both being enrolled at the Royal College of Music. A friendly rivalry had turned into something with more bite to it when their careers as professional artists had taken off and Jules's undoubted superiority had caused a hardness tinged with petulance to take hold of Boris, which Jules had noticed with dismay.

10

The hall filled to capacity and Jules was summoned to start. He could scarcely hear the applause when he entered but he could see his parents staring eagerly up at him. He steadied himself and began. He needed no page-turner. He was master of the pieces and, after the first few bars, his fingers flew with the notes.

In the hall an unease developed, like the first hint of infidelity in a stable marriage. Bodies shuffled and enquiring heads were turned on each other. This disquiet slowly welled up like an overburdened reservoir, the restraints faltering until something gave way.

Jack Stringer, music critic of *The Times*, suddenly left the hall.

Outside the manager anxiously accosted him. 'What's happening Jack?'

'I'll tell you what's happening. I'm off. I'm not staying here to listen to such caterwauling.'

'What on earth do you mean, caterwauling? Young Jules is one of the best pianists we've got, and you know it.'

'He isn't tonight, I can tell you. Just go in and listen. Might I suggest your piano is out of tune?'

'That's unheard of,' said Franco indignantly. 'It's always carefully tuned before every concert.'

' "Unheard of" about sums it up for me. It will be unheard of by me. No, I tell a lie. It will be bruited abroad by me in tomorrow's paper. Is Jules Osk so incompetent that he cannot hear the noise he is making? Yes noise! Nothing more. It's an affront to the Wigmore Hall and the concert-going public. Old Bechenstein must be turning in his grave.' He strode out.

Franco turned to find a stream of discontented patrons leaving. He glanced in at the hall. Jules was still playing away but Franco could now hear the sounds of the piano and he froze with horror. Instead of the cadances he knew so well, alien harmonies and sequences were coming from the piano. Subtle alterations of pitch completely disintegrated the progression of the music and, by denying what it promised, awakened a feeling of distress in the hearer, like a hungry man who dives in with his fork to his favourite roast, only to find it has been burnt to a bitter, acrid flavour.

11

He was not aware of Jules's deafness. Jules had, naturally enough, aimed to conceal the fact for as long as was possible. Only his family and close associates like Boris were aware of his affliction.

Boris was still in his seat. Franco noticed a strange look on his face. Whereas the prevailing attitude was of concern and dismay, Boris seemed to be smiling inwardly. His thin, angular body was rapt, craning forward in his seat, and every so often he turned his head round to watch the audience, most of whom by now had left or were in the process of leaving. It was at these moments that Franco particularly noticed what he could only think of as a smirk on Boris's face.

Mr and Mrs Osk were still in their places but were fidgeting and ill at ease.

Jules came to the end of the first movement and paused. Peter moved his head and shoulders in a gesture trying to draw Jules's attention, but Jules was sitting, breathing deeply, his hands resting on his knees.

'We must stop him,' Peter whispered to Mary.

'You can't make a fuss now.'

'I must, if needs be. There's enough fuss already. Everyone's leaving. There's something wrong with that damn piano and poor old Jules doesn't hear it. We've got to tell him. Maybe it can be put right.'

Jules showed signs of starting the second movement. Franco was staring agitatedly at the platform and then became caught up in conversation with the outflow of disgruntled critics and patrons.

Peter rose suddenly and tiptoed up the steps to the dais. Jules glanced round, startled. His plump face, with its prominent nose and expressive hazel eyes, showed alarm. What's the matter, it said?

'Jules, there's something wrong with the piano. It's out of tune I think.'

Although Peter spoke into Jules's ear, Jules could not hear and Peter had to raise his voice. He repeated his remark more loudly, and gestured to Jules towards the emptying hall. Jules looked down at the auditorium for the first time. He took in the horror of the exodus.

'What's gone wrong Dad? Did you say the piano was out of tune? Why are they all leaving? Can't you stop them? I can't have been as bad as all that. Stop them.'

He pushed his stool back and ran down into the hall.

'Where are they all going? Surely it can be put right, whatever it is? Boris, what's going on? Please tell me.' He ran over to his friend.

Boris got up and patted Jules on the shoulder. His face, lean and pointed, in contrast to Jules's, showed concern.

'I don't know why they are all leaving Jules. The piano wasn't sounding too good, but you did your best.' He smiled.

Jules had been lip reading and Boris, with the rest of Jules's friends and family, had acquired the habit of enunciating their words so that Jules could pick up what they said.

'Obviously my best was not good enough. Look at them all, streaming out. What can I do, I'm ruined.'

Peter and Mary came over. Franco had still not disentangled himself from the audience.

Mary took hold of Jules's hands and squeezed them tightly. She pulled on them when Jules made to move away.

'There was something wrong with that piano. It made a horrible sound. It wasn't your fault dear.'

'I'm going to see the manager,' said Peter Osk with determination.

He strode over to where Franco was still remonstrating with his dissatisfied clientele. He caught Franco by the arm and swung him round with the vigour of indignation.

'Mr Paster, I want an explanation for tonight's fiasco.'

'So do I, Mr Osk. So do I.'

'The piano cannot have been tuned. It's disgraceful.'

'It was tuned. It's always tuned. We would not permit otherwise.'

'But it obviously wasn't. Anyone could hear that.'

'Well, in that case, why didn't your son draw our attention to it? Even if he had stopped after the first few bars it would have been better than this. Much better. This is a fiasco.'

Peter paused. Was now the time to reveal Jules's handicap? He went over to his son, who was arguing with the last few

13

patrons on their way out. He seemed to be pleading with them to stay, and caught hold of the sleeve of one of them. His hands were pulled away by another and the last few left.

'Jules. You must listen.' Peter spoke clearly.

'Listen! That's just what I can't do, isn't it. Listen. Are you trying to rub it in Dad? Haven't I suffered enough for one day? My whole future's ruined.'

Jules clenched his fists and paced down towards the piano, gazing up at the arched ceiling. The large central glass panel was dark by now. Mary approached him tentatively and paused. Then she hugged him to her. Jules's head jutted over her shoulder and he glanced again at the ceiling.

'My future's just like that ceiling; dark.'

Jules looked at his father with eyes which reminded Peter of the time Jules's pet rabbit had died; eyes full of profound despair which had appeared round the door one Saturday morning and had torn Peter's heartstrings apart.

He patted his son gently on the back when Mary released her hold, and all three stood irresolute.

Franco Paster came up at that moment.

'Jules, I cannot say how sorry I am about tonight. Why did you go on? There must have been something wrong with the piano. You should have stopped.'

Jules was in the mood to come clean about his deafness. They all might as well know, he thought. It can't be worse than what happens when they don't know.

'I didn't stop Franco for the very good reason that I didn't hear it. You see I am rather deaf and what with that and my concentration I just didn't notice.'

'If you could only judge a performance by the handiwork you were magnificent,' Peter put in.

'If only I had known,' sighed Franco, 'I could have done something about it.'

'Yes, probably never have engaged me. That was my worry. Still is my worry.'

Franco sensed a marketing opportunity.

'Do you mind if we put out a press release as to what has happened, giving the reasons of course?'

14

'Go ahead. Let it all hang out. It might as well now. Does that mean you would not be averse to engaging me again?'

'Certainly, young man. And I will personally ensure that the piano is in spanking condition.'

'If it isn't you'll be in a spanking situation, I can tell you.'

They all had relaxed by this time. Boris had disappeared and the hall was empty apart from two members of the staff who were tidying up.

'I still can't make out what happened to that piano?' Franco frowned. 'It has never let us down before. I shall check with the tuner in the morning and let you know.'

The Osks arrived back at their house earlier than expected. Their neighbours had been aware of Jules's important assignation and were alert to the family's return.

Fletcher Pemberton, their closest neighbour, was in his late forties. His chief characteristic was an insatiable curiosity about how things worked which he had turned into a commercial asset by becoming a much-sought-after restorer of organs. Doris, his wife, bore his foibles with fortitude and his frequent absences in the course of his duties with resignation not unmixed with relief. At such times, Mary observed, Doris would be seen with a blithe swing in her stride and, she fancied, a song in her heart.

'What song?' Peter would ask. 'Absence makes the heart grow fonder?'

'That's no song. That's an apopthegm.'

'There are a lot of "Ps" and diphthongs in that.'

'You mind your "Ps" and "Qs". You're not doing so badly in the diphthong stakes yourself.'

They had barely settled in on their return before Fletcher came round, his rufous face peering in as he approached the front door. He was stocky, with big ears and hands, and possessed a slightly crooked nose which tended to give him a quizzical look, which he used to advantage on occasion.

'Hello. You're back early.' He stood on the threshold, implacable with curiosity.

Mary had answered the door and was not quite sure whether Jules would welcome any visitor after his tribulations.

'Yes, we are.' She hesitated. Fletcher was not one to fail to perceive the nuances of life.

'Something amiss? Would you rather I left?'

Just then Jules emerged from the sitting-room and noticed Fletcher.

'Hello Fletcher. Have you heard the wretched thing which happened to me today? My concert was a flop. A big resounding flop.'

Fletcher came into the hall. 'Why on earth? What happened then?'

'You had better come and sit down for a moment.'

Mary decided Jules was in a mood to talk about the episode and get it off his chest.

Jules related all.

Fletcher already knew of his deafness. 'But that's extraordinary. Their piano tuner needs a good kick in the pants. And his tuning fork to follow you know where,' he added. 'Pianos don't go out of tune to that degree on their own, not in my view. Someone must have tampered with it. There's no other explanation to my mind.'

'Tampered with it? Who on earth would want to do that?' Mary asked.

'Find that out and you've probably got your answer. A rival perhaps. It seems absurd but there's a lot of competition about. Tricks of the trade, that's probably what they would call it. A sort of industrial espionage if you like, putting a bomb under someone's car because you differ with their politics. It's all the same these days.'

'Put like that, what's happened to me doesn't seem too heinous a crime.' Jules had been lip reading carefully. 'Puts it in perspective really.'

'What are you going to do about it? That's the point'.

'I shall carry on as long as I am wanted. And jolly well make sure that the piano is in tune before I start. That's what I'm going to do. I want a well tempered clavier, not a well tampered one.'

16

'Good lad,' Peter added. 'And we'll make a few enquiries tomorrow about who had access to that piano before the concert.'

'We certainly will.' Jules rose from his chair, closed one hand over the other fist and paced the room.

'I just can't believe that anyone would stoop so low. It seems incredible.'

'Unfortunately it's all too credible. There's an ethos abroad that it is up to everyone to fend for himself, and no holds barred. Anything goes in love and war. That sort of thing. But I must go. You'll be wanting to forget today, erase it from the slate.' Fletcher prepared to leave.

'No. I shall not forget today. I shall store it in me and use it as fuel. I shan't let it poison me or rot my guts. I shall draw on it when I want stiffening.' Jules gazed excitedly at them.

Mary smiled in her own quiet way and the men nodded approvingly.

'If there's anything in *The Times* do you want me to bring it round?'

'Yes please. I'll be interested to read what they say about it.'

'I don't expect it will be in tomorrow. More likely the next day.' Fletcher went off home.

The next day Franco had the piano checked and found that some of the notes were indeed out of tune. His enquiries elicited the information that the piano tuner, who was adamant that he had left the piano in perfect working order, had completed his task an hour before the concert. In that hour intervening before the start several members of the staff had been about but none had entered the concert hall.

The booking staff had noted a young man who went in quite early. He had seemed to know what he was doing and where to go and they had not thought it necessary to tell the security officer. They could not say for sure where he went or what happened to him, and were unable to describe him other than that he was a young fellow, possibly in his twenties, quite small

17

and with dark hair.

Franco did not consider this description sufficient to pin down anyone he knew and when Peter rang him he gave the information in a dismissive way.

'I don't think we are going to get much endeavour from our Mr Paster over this one,' Peter observed.

A little germ of suspicion stirred in Jules's mind. He envisaged Boris sitting at the end of the row during the fiasco, when everyone else was milling about and preparing to leave. There had been something about his expression which, now that Jules came to consider it, was not quite right. Whereas the others all manifested concern and tribulation in various degrees, Boris had seemed to emanate a different feeling, almost one of quiet satisfaction, Jules thought. There had been the ghost of a smile on his face and when he had come over to express concern it had seemed a surface show without depth. Jules decided to keep his thoughts to himself for the time being.

The next day Fletcher came round with *The Times*.

'Are you sure you want to read it? It won't please you, I'm afraid.'

'Well, everyone else is going to read it so I might as well.' Jules sighed. 'At least I'll know what I'm up against.'

The notice was headlined 'Unprecedented Fiasco at The Wigmore Hall' by Jack Stringer. Jules read on. 'The piano recital by Jules Osk which should have taken place at the Wigmore Hall last evening was abandoned after the first movement of the opening Beethoven Sonata. The discordant notes which were heard were too much for the sophisticated audience to tolerate and the concert was abandoned in turmoil.

'That such a disaster should be allowed to take place reflects severe and condign criticism on all those concerned, and in particular on the pianist himself. Whatever the respective responsibilities of the Wigmore Hall authorities and the artist it is the artist himself, in the ultimate, who must bear the blame for perpetrating such an outrage on the concert-going public.

If Jules Osk had been unable to ensure that his instrument was in good working order, and there will be those who say that there can be no excuse, he should, at least, have brought his

18

deplorable performance to a halt when he perceived that all was not well with the piano. Who would willingly submit himself to a surgeon who did not ensure that his knives were sharp?

This young lad's future must be in doubt. There are some mistakes which cannot be remedied.'

'Phew!' exclaimed Jules. 'He didn't pull his punches and there is a sting in the tail.'

'Pen dipped in venom, or vitriol, I would say.'

'Are you going to make a reply to Jack Stringer?' Fletcher enquired.

'What do you think?' Jules looked round at them all.

'There's a risk of starting a sort of chain reaction, contumely piled on contumely,' Peter said.

'You would have to think carefully before getting embroiled,' Mary said quietly, 'but on the whole I feel a dignified reply might be a sound idea.'

'I'll go along with that,' Peter added. They all turned to Jules.

'Yes. I would like to make some sort of reply, restrained and yet forceful, if one can combine those two qualities. I think I have little to lose now in making public knowledge of my increasing deafness. It might, in fact, get me some public sympathy and interest, always providing my standard of play is up to the mark. That goes without saying. Let's all four of us make up our own contribution and then compare them and sort out the best from each.'

They all settled down to write.

When they had finished they looked at Jules.

'Well here goes: "Dear sir, I hope you will do me the courtesy of printing my reply to the criticisms of your Music Correspondent levelled at me in today's issue of your paper.

First of all I would point out that I suffer from increasing deafness. I therefore did not hear that the piano was out of tune. One might expect that would be properly tuned on such an occasion. How this was not so remains, at the moment, a mystery.

I have every intention of continuing my career as long as possible, in spite of your critic's misgivings." '

19

The others read out their contributions and a synthesis of the best bits was assembled into the final draft.

That afternoon Jules decided to confront Boris.

'Where are you off to?' Mary called out.

'Just going shopping. I'll be back for supper.'

Jules had ascertained that Boris would be at home that afternoon at Chase Farm and by three o'clock he was ringing at the door. He had no clear notion how he would go about things when he saw him, preferring to leave it to the impulse of the moment.

2

Mrs Striman opened the door. Jules thought he could hear the sound of a piano in the background.

'Hello Mrs Striman. Would it be possible for me to have a word with Boris?'

Mrs Striman hesitated. 'He is practising, you know. I expect you can hear him. I don't like interrupting him during his practice.'

'There's something important I want to say to him. I don't think he'll mind.'

Mrs Striman recognised determination when she encountered it. 'All right. You know your way, I think.'

Jules knocked on the door, paused for a moment and then entered. Boris looked up from the piano and his eyes widened. A flit of anxiety showed.

'Hello Jules. To what do I owe the honour?' He stood up and came over to him. He started to grasp his arm but Jules shrugged him off.

'I want to go over what happened the other night Boris. You were there, were you not?'

'You know I was. You jolly well saw me. I'm terribly sorry about what happened. Take a seat, Jules.'

Jules was watching Boris's lips closely so as not to miss a word.

'Are you sorry about what happened? Perhaps you are and perhaps you aren't. Who knows?'

'What do you mean by that?' Boris tried to summon indignation to his aid but found it difficult.

'Well, we are rivals in a way. Someone had tampered with that piano, I'm sure of that.'

'It certainly sounded awful. I didn't realise you were as deaf as that and did not hear it.'

'Would not hear it or did not hear it. Which do you mean? Is is possible you mean I "would" not hear it. Had this thought already occurred to you before the concert? It certainly sounded like it from what you have just said.'

'I can't remember exactly what I said now. I meant I didn't think you were as deaf as all that.'

'I am going to get to the bottom of it. Did you know that a dark-complexioned young man was noticed by some staff going into the premises about half-an-hour before the start of the performance? Does that surprise you in any way?'

Jules stared fixedly at Boris and felt anger mounting within him.

Boris swallowed and his prominent Adam's apple rode up and down.

'There must have been lots of dark-complexioned young men in the audience that night. Are you suggesting it might have been me?'

'The thought did occur. In fact it still occurs, more and more forcibly, now I see you.'

'Why do you say that?' Boris was aware that he cut an unfortunate picture just then but could not summon himself into a more assertive mood.

'I'm going to take you down to the Wigmore Hall and ask if any of the staff remember a young man who went in early looking anything like you. What were you wearing? Yes, I remember, grey flannels and a maroon polo-neck sweater. You can jolly well put them on and come down with me.' Jules stood over Boris.

'Keep off me,' Boris shouted. 'I'm certainly not going to do as you say. It's ridiculous.'

'What's all the shouting.' The door opened and Mr Striman came in. 'What's going on?'

'Dad, Jules was going to attack me.'

Jules stood back. 'I merely asked Boris to come down to the

22

Wigmore Hall with me.'

'What on earth for? Why should he if he doesn't want to? What's all this about?' Mr Striman looked menacing.

'I expect you have heard what happened at my concert the other night, Mr Striman. Well, someone had tampered with the piano and members of the staff saw a dark young man enter about half-an-hour beforehand. It's more than likely that that chap altered the tuning of the piano. Someone must have done so, pianos don't alter that much on their own and the tuner, whom I know well, is adamant that he left the piano in good order an hour before the concert.' Jules paused to take breath.

'Well he could have been mistaken,' said Mr Striman. 'That's far more likely, to my mind, than that some idiot would deliberately tamper with the wretched instrument.'

'It's not the instrument who is wretched, but me. I'm wretched and also determined to find out. Find out I will.' Jules started again at Boris. 'Are you coming with me?'

'No, I'm not.'

'I'm afraid you are.' Jules started to haul Boris up from his chair.

Mr Striman aimed a blow at Jules which Jules half parried. 'You get out of my house at once.'

Mrs Striman now appeared. 'What are you men all up to? Great goofs. Behave yourselves.'

'Jules is just leaving,' said Mr Striman.

Jules hesitated and decided he would get no further that day.

'You'll hear more of this. I shan't let it drop.'

'And you'll hear from my solicitor for causing a disturbance in my house, refusing to leave when asked and for defamation.'

☆ ☆ ☆

Jules arranged to see his own family solicitor the next afternoon without mentioning any of this to his parents. They had noticed his preoccupation.

'Jules doesn't seem quite himself,' Peter observed when he had gone out.

'I think this piano business is preying on his mind.'

'It's not surprising really. After all, it is his whole life, music; has become so, anyway.'

'That's what I don't like about modern life.' Mary frowned. 'Every activity seems to have to be so intense.'

'Yes, and that leads to obsession. And aggression,' Peter added, 'No room for the inspired amateur now. The Corinthian days are over.'

'Corinthian columns are out and concrete columns are in, in position.'

'Yes. And they don't look so good, do they. Now you come to think of it, modern architecture reflects modern thought, doesn't it. Functional and tough. No room for embellishments or curlicues.'

'Unendurable, I would say.'

They awaited Jules's return with niggling anxiety. The umbilical cord is never wholly severed, Mary thought. Only attenuated and frayed. Very frayed at times.

☆ ☆ ☆

Meanwhile Jules was in Frank Barstow's office. Mr Barstow looked the part, or had become to look the part of a family solicitor. He was dapper, neat and precise, with a sharp, alert face and hands which fluttered deprecatingly from time to time.

'What is the problem, Jules?' Mr Barstow folded his hands before him on the desk.

Jules waited for them to flutter again at any minute. He related the circumstances and finished with a request that Boris should be made to appear before the Wigmore staff on an identity parade.

'At the moment he refuses.'

Mr Barstow's face twisted momentarily in a smile, but it was gone in an instant.

'We often find, under such circumstances, that a letter threatening to invoke the law works wonders.'

'If that's what you advise then I'll go along with that.'

'Excellent.' Hands rubbed in approval, deprecation being inappropriate. 'I shall inform you when you can expect the letter to be delivered.'

'And then I shall have another go at him. Thank you Mr Barstow.'

3

Fletcher, in the course of his endeavours among the gilded pipes
and ivory keyboards of his church organs, had often mused on
the cadances of the birds which he would hear through the
stained-glass windows, so frequently infracted. At times the
cascade would halt his mallet in mid-air and he would remain
poised on his steps, as if embalmed in the sound.

He decided that now was the time to study bird-song a little,
enlisting the help of Jules and thereby giving the lad some fresh
purpose after his tribulations. He had not fully understood the
degree of Jules's deafness when the notion had first taken him,
but felt, this handicap notwithstanding, he would pursue the
plan.

He was round at the Osks' bright and early the next morning.

'I want to enlist your aid, Jules, in a little project which I have
cherished to my bosom for some time. I know your hearing is
not good, but you can still help me enormously if you are
willing.'

'What on earth does it involve?'

'It involves getting up early in the morning, when the dawn
chorus is full-throated and resonant, taken at the flood, recording the note sequences and intervals, and then sounding a note
from the church organ to see whether it has any effect on the
birds. That's where you come in mainly, to give the steady note
on the organ.'

Jules surprised Fletcher by launching forth into a long quota-
tion.

27

'There is a tide in the affairs of men,
Which, taken at the flood, leads on to fortune,
Omitted, all the voyage of their life
Is bound in shallows and miseries,
On such a full sea are we now afloat,
And we must take the current when it serves,
Or lose our ventures.'

Jules grinned at Fletcher and tilted his head. Fletcher raised his eyebrows. 'Do I take it that is "Yes"?'
'Yes.'

☆ ☆ ☆

The following morning the two figures were to be seen walking down to the church. Each wore an anorak; mufflers couched their necks against the fresh morning air which showed the steam of their breaths. They carried recording equipment and Fletcher swung the massive church key from his wrist.

Trees surrounded the church and Fletcher selected a mountain ash, between the entrance gate and the south porch which he had noted was a popular rendezvous with the birds. They stowed their apparatus near the tree and unlocked the church. Inside it was chill and musty. The morning light shone through the stained glass windows and the colours shone with the conviction of their beauty.

Jules located the organ and was about to try out a few notes. Fletcher restrained him. 'Not yet, Jules. First I want to get the bird-notes, bird-pitches, call them what you will, before you play your note, and then again after you have sounded. What note do you think best?'

'It's not a matter I had given much thought until now, but since the time has come for a decision, I suggest the G above middle C and then a higher and lower G.'

'Right. We'll go and set up the equipment. There's a ladder in the vestry. I'll go and get it.'

All went well while the recordings were made of the natural bird-song. Then Jules was dispatched to sound his steady G.

28

The note joined the chorus of sounds with dignity and played amongst the trees and birds, and echoed softly off the tombstones. Fletcher nodded approvingly. He heard an alien whistling down the road and ran out of the gateway waving his arms.

The postman braked his bike in astonishment. 'What's got into you? Have you seen a ghost in the churchyard?'

'Shush.' Fletcher placed a finger to his lips.

'I don't think there is anyone in there who is going to hear what we say.'

'No, no. You don't understand. We are recording the birds.'

'What birds? I can't see any, not my sort anyway.' The postman grinned.

'Do be quiet. Please.'

The postman pretended to ring his bell and Fletcher grabbed his hand to stop him.

The Alsatian, which had been loping along behind the bike and was now sprawled on the road, leapt up and snarled; then it let out a ferocious bark and showed its fangs.

Fletcher wiped his brow in a gesture of resignation. Jules's G sounded sonorously from the church but the cascades of birdsong had faltered in the face of the Alsatian's barks and the scuffles on the road.

'Well, I'll leave you to your chirrups and yaffles.' The postman mounted his bike and called to his dog. 'Come on Pouncer. Oh, sorry. Quite forgot. Hush, hush the order of the day.'

Just then the milk float trundled by. The vehicle hit a pothole in the road and all the milk-bottles jangled together in a chorus of disapproval. The milkman bellowed a greeting to the postman as he passed.

'That's the last straw,' Fletcher told the heavens with emphasis. He went into the church. Jules saw him coming and showed signs of relief.

'I was wondering how long you wanted me to go on. I don't know if a single note can wear out but this G must believe it's been entered for the marathon.'

Fletcher grinned and bowed low. 'The air on a G string can

take a break,' he pronounced, mouthing the words.

Jules removed his finger with a flourish.

Fletcher spoke earnestly to Jules, facing him fully.

'The experiment has not been entirely successful, I'm afraid, owing to certain extraneous noises which I encountered, to whit the postman and his dog, and subsequently the milkman and his entourage of bottles, many of whom seemed intent on signifying their presence as they passed.'

'At least you made no mention of Concorde passing over. That would have lifted things onto a higher plane.'

'Bother the birds, I'll have another go sometime. Think it out a bit more first though.'

4

A few days later Peter was reading the paper when the phone rang. He went to answer. It was Mr Barstow. Jules had told his parents of his visit.

'Will you kindly inform Jules that my letter should have arrived at the Striman household this morning. It has suggested, gently but firmly, that legal proceedings will be initiated if Boris Striman does not present himself for the Wigmore Hall staff to inspect him. May I leave Jules to follow this up and report back to me in due course?'

'You may Mr Barstow. And thank you.'

When Jules came in Peter told him of the call and Jules decided to visit Boris's home once more.

'Shall I come with you?' Peter asked.

'No Dad. Thanks all the same. I think it's best if I can sort it out with Boris myself.'

Mrs Striman answered the door. She frowned. 'Oh. It's you.' She hesitated.

'Can I see Boris please. Is he in?'

'Yes, he's in. I don't know if he'll see you though. Wait a minute.'

Jules stood uneasily on the threshold and smelt coffee. It was the only thing which seemed normal today, he mused. Apart from that everything had an unreal quality, rather like a dream, and a dream of which he had little control. Mrs Striman returned.

'Come in.' She stood aside and Jules entered.

He saw Boris come into the hall. Boris stood back awkwardly

neither smiling nor frowning, impassive. His eyes were trained on Jules.

'Boris, have you received a letter from my solicitor?' Boris stood motionless. 'Well, have you?'

Jules could see Boris's lips move but failed to hear the low assent. Boris spoke up, with a sudden infusion of animus.

'Yes I have. Was it really necessary? A bit over the top I should have thought. If you really want me to take part in such a ridiculous charade then I suppose I must, but you didn't need to go to these lengths. I'll come any time you want. Right now if you wish.'

His eyes flashed defiance and for a moment Jules was taken aback. Then the remembrance of his humiliation hit him.

'Right-o. We'll go now. Come on.'

'Don't you think you ought to consult your father first?' Mrs Striman said anxiously, but she knew she was addressing a closed door.

'Leave this to me Mother. It's got to be settled.'

Their journey by tube to the Wigmore Hall was conducted in an aura of punctilious hostility. The few words Boris addressed to Jules were spoken with exaggerated deliberation as if to emphasise Jules's deafness.

Jules attempted to dowse the fires of resentment flaming deep within him, but every so often they flared up and he could feel a twitching of his facial muscles and a tautening of his fingers.

Both men were relieved when they at last walked in and approached the reception desk. Driven respectively by anger and defiance neither had felt like checking whether the appropriate people were available on that day.

'Could we see Mr Paster please?' Jules enquired.

'He's in his office. Who shall I say wants to see him?'

'Jules Osk.'

Mr Paster appeared.

'Hello Jules. Glad to see you. I hope you have got over the other evening; most unfortunate.' His look wandered to Boris. 'Is this Boris Striman? I think I am right.'

'Pretty good of you to recognise me.'

'It's my job to recognise our musicians. After all, they provide my bread and butter, don't they.'

'Not always,' said Jules. 'Sometimes it's wormwood and gall.'

'Yes the other night was very galling.' He laughed but the others did not join in.

Mr Paster cleared his throat. 'What did you wish to see me about?'

'Well it's rather private.'

'You had better come into my office then.'

When they were seated Jules explained.

'You know some of your staff said they saw a young fellow come into the hall on the night of my concert, concert to be, that is. Well I wondered if Boris here might have been the one they saw. He has agreed to come along and let them see if the chap looked like him.'

Boris was silent for a while. Then he said, 'I can't remember exactly what time I arrived, I'm afraid. Sorry.'

'Well we can soon settle that.' Mr Paster rose and went towards the door. 'The two staff concerned are here right now. I'll just go and get them, if you'll excuse me.'

Boris looked with a steady hostility at Jules but kept his silence.

Jules now felt doubts about the whole thing. Even if the chap had been Boris, who's to say whether he interfered with the piano? Boris's stare made him falter.

'At least if they say it was you they saw it will rule out any other chap.' Jules tried to smile. 'So that will be something, won't it?'

Boris's expression maintained it's venom. 'And if they do identify me what does that prove?'

'Well nothing really, I suppose.'

Boris sensed an ascendency. 'Do you seriously maintain that I might have tampered with your piano?' He snorted and turned away.

Just then Mr Paster returned with the two staff. The girls stood close together near the doorway and seemed inclined to giggle. He explained what was required of them.

'This is serious, you know. Please consider the matter carefully.'

33

The girls looked at Boris and pursed their lips, partly to appear serious and partly to disown incipient smiles. They shook their heads simultaneously.

'Do you recognise him as the man who came in early or don't you?' Mr Paster allowed an aggrieved note to enter into his enquiry.

'Can't say,' said one of them.

'Nor can I,' said the other. There was a pause.

'Is that all you have got to say then?'

They giggled.

'That seems to settle that,' said Boris, making no attempt to conceal a note of triumph. 'If the piano was tampered with it certainly wasn't me.' He stood up.

Jules had not been able to hear completely but realised the general import. He realised that he would get no further with the matter.

'Thank you Mr Paster, and the girls too.' He smiled wanly and slowly shook his head.

Compassion was stirred in Boris and softened his lineaments, as compassion can do; the sharpness of his features rounded and mellowed by some slight lessening of muscular tension, the furrows on his face softened and lightened and his hand opened out almost imperceptibly as the shoulders drooped.

'Come on Jules. Let's be off.'

5

Both Jules and Boris sang on Sundays in a prestigious church in Mayfair. So far Jules's deafness had not encroached on his capacities in that direction.

Also in the choir was Fiona Blake, who flouted the usual mutual exclusion between plumpness and liveliness by possessing both attributes in generous measure. She had a sallow complexion, dark curly hair and green eyes which could flash and blaze with her mood, and put Jules in mind of:

> '*Tyger, Tyger! Burning bright*
> *In the forests of the night,*
> *What immortal hand or eye*
> *Could frame thy fearful symmetry?*
> *In what distant deeps or skies*
> *Burnt the fire of thine eyes?*'

Jules had taken her out to one or two concerts and films and she had read with distress the notice in *The Times* of Jules's abortive concert. This Sunday was the first since then when they had met.

She commiserated with Jules as they were preparing for the service and her eyes spoke to him in tones which reached the depths of his being.

'Come over to my place and tell me all about it. It's my half-day on Wednesday. Come over for tea.'

'That would be fine. See you then.'

After that Jules sang the refrains and hymns with conviction and when Fiona smiled across the aisle his heart leapt with joy. Wednesday could not come too soon.

The Blakes lived in a rambling house near Epping Forest and possessed a garden the extent of which ambled here and there on the edge of the forest. In places garden and forest seemed to have agreed to link hands and merge identities, an arrangement which suited Gilbert Blake admirably. No one could recall when the Christian name 'Gilbert' had been adopted but there was a family tradition that his long-established love of the ways of Rev. Gilbert White of Selborne had caused the switch from Wilfred to Gilbert, a substitution which Mr Blake by no means deplored. He was a chunky, muscular man, with the same dark features as Fiona, but a redder face, probably due to the considerable amount of time he spent out in his beloved garden.

Marigold Blake, in contrast, was rather thin and droopy, with a quizzical sense of humour, an attribute which came in handy with her family, as she frequently observed.

Fiona had only mentioned her father's interests in vague terms to Jules. The extent of these interests was manifest as Jules walked up the drive. On the front lawn stood a miscellany of objects answering to the general description of '-ometers' of one sort or another. He thought he recognised the white, louvred box-like structure of a rain gauge and the hollow object revolving gracefully on the end of a long pole must be some sort of wind gauge, he surmised. The purpose of other objects on display was more obscure.

Fiona had been expecting him and answered the door when he rang. She was wearing an apple green dress with a salmon-coloured pattern of flowers. The freshness and allure of young girls in the spring struck Jules forcibly. After introductions to Marigold, her mother, and her two brothers, Fiona took Jules out to the back garden. She spotted her father embroiled with the intricacies of one of his gadgets.

'Dad. Hold on a minute. This is Jules. He plays the piano. You remember, I was telling you about him.'

36

Gilbert shook Jules warmly by the hand. He was wearing a green boiler suit much lived in so that it rode comfortably over his contours.

'I believe I have to speak up a bit to make you hear.'

'I'm afraid that's true. I'm a bit deaf. Well, rather deaf actually.' Jules smiled sheepishly.

'Never mind. We're all deaf, and blind, in a sort of way. When you come to think of how much we fail to see and hear that is going on around us it makes me, well, despair. There are more than enough sensations, beautiful sensations, ready for us to receive if only we were receptive. But we're not, that's the trouble. We're worried about the income tax or the spot on our chin.' He glanced at Fiona and grinned.

'Get off your hobbyhorse Dad.'

Gilbert laughed out loud. 'I'd sooner be on a hobby-horse than shanks's pony. Shanks's pony would be better than nothing though. Honestly Jules, it's as if we were seated with a beautiful book on the table beside us and all we did was notice that the spine was worn or one of the pages torn, but never read the book.'

Jules saw the sense in what Gilbert was saying. 'Our neighbour would love to meet you.'

Jules outlined their attempts to monitor bird-song and Gilbert listened with rapt attention.

'I certainly would love to meet this chap. Sounds a man after my own heart.'

'Both need your heads examined, more like,' Fiona laughed. 'I suppose you are going to insist on showing Jules your set up.'

'Since you mention it, and in short, yes.'

He grabbed Jules by the arm and bore him off. Fiona shook her head slowly in mock resignation and went in to chat with her mother and prepare some tea.

'Gilbert White, the Rev. Gilbert White of Selborne,' Gilbert said, being careful to mouth his words so that Jules could follow, 'kept these meticulous records of all the little happenings in nature. For instance, and I quote, "Feb. 2, Brown wood-owls hoot, Feb. 3, Hens sit, marsh titmouse begins his two sharp notes, Feb. 4, Gossamer floats and Musca Tenax appears, Feb. 7,

Foxes smell rank, Feb. 10, Turkey cocks strut and gobble, Feb. 12, Yellowhammer sings, Feb. 13, Green Woodpecker laughs, Feb. 14, Ravens build," and so on.'

Gilbert drew a deep breath and held his hand open as if to say 'What more could you want?'

'I thought we did the gobbling not the turkey cocks.'

'They gobble out and we gobble up. There's a deal of difference in a preposition. Just think of the excitement White must have felt each morning when he woke, anticipating what the day would bring him.'

They toured the garden.

'You've got just about every type of gauge here except the greengage.'

'Giving me a raspberry for that, are you young man?' Gilbert pushed Jules playfully.

Jules stumbled on a piece of apparatus and fell gracefully onto some nettles. He got up ruefully and rubbed his hands, which had been stung.

'Should those be there?' he said playfully. 'A trap for the unwary.'

'They are not a deliberate mistake or even the fruits of idleness. I let them grow to punish interlopers who stumble over my stuff.' He smiled. 'No, seriously. They are to encourage certain species of insect.'

'Such as Musca Tenax. I was going to ask you what it was.'

'All right, you'll do.'

Just then they heard Fiona summon them for tea.

When they were seated Jules viewed with trepidation the array of homemade bread, scones and cakes. He realised why Fiona's figure was nourished so generously in the midst of such nutritional temptation, a temptation shared willingly by Fiona's two brothers, who erupted from nowhere with vigour and, after brief introductions, set to on the food with equal determination and more application.

Marigold viewed the scene with evident satisfaction, seated at the head of the table with an expression of Buddha-like impassivity and contentment.

'Gilbert has his little domain outside and mine is here, within.'

'It's certainly not without,' Jules laughed. He pretended to look under the table.

'What are you up to, Jules?' Fiona asked.

'I'm looking for the kitchen sink. There's everything here except the kitchen sink, so I thought it might be hiding under the table.'

'You'll get a hiding if you make remarks like that,' Gilbert said.

He pretended to wince with pain and rubbed his foot.

'Now, what are you up to?' Marigold asked.

'I've just stubbed my toe.'

'How can you? On what?'

'On the kitchen sink, of course.'

'Any more of that from either of you and you'll both be sent out among the birds and bees.'

'Oooooh. That'll be nice,

"Where the bee sucks there suck I
In a cowslip's bell I lie,
There I couch when owls do cry."

'They won't be the only things crying,' said Marigold.

She filled the cups with a flourish of the teapot, which was ornately decorated with a picture of bees pursuing a man from the environs of their hive.

'That's a most extraordinary teapot,' Jules exclaimed.

'It is. And the person wielding it is much the same,' said Gilbert.

'Do you mean there's a sting in her tail?' one of the boys put in.

'I remember when we got that.' Marigold looked reminiscent. 'We were on holiday in Sussex, do you remember? We had gone to buy some honey from that little shop in the country and saw this set. We got the honey pot and this teapot.'

'Yes, and some honey,' Fiona added. 'I can remember the mess the boys made when they got into the honey on our way back in the car.'

'They've been in a mess ever since,' Gilbert laughed.

'Dad, that's not fair!' they chorused.

'That's one time, probably the only time, when they both agree,' Fiona said, shaking her head, 'when they're under attack.'

'No it isn't,' Marigold added. 'When it's time for bed, that's another time.'

After tea Fiona and Jules set off for a walk. They chatted of this and that but Jules found it difficult to hear Fiona's soft voice, especially as he could not see the movement of her lips without craning round at her.

Their easeful contentment slipped away as the light slowly faded and a note of exasperation crept into their talk.

Fiona could feel herself becoming more and more irritated.

'It's very awkward having to speak so distinctly.' The moment she had uttered this she regretted it.

For once Jules had heard clearly, in the way that cutting remarks have of making their presence felt. He felt too numb to reply and walked on in silence, slightly quickening his pace.

After a little while he stopped, turned and said rather harshly, 'We had better get back now I think.' He did not look at Fiona.

'I'm sorry Jules. I didn't mean it. I didn't mean to hurt you.' She waited. 'It was beastly of me. Please don't be so upset.' But she knew it was too late.

They walked back in silence. Jules went in to thank his hosts and prepared to leave.

'Shall I walk with you to the bus stop?' Fiona asked, holding his arm lightly.

'No thank you. I'll be off now.' He left without another word.

Fiona plonked herself down on a kitchen chair.

'I don't think that walk did either of you much good, did it?' Marigold was just finishing the washing-up. Fiona explained.

'I'm afraid handicaps are handicaps. There's no getting away from it. I wish there were.'

Marigold gazed out of the window where Gilbert was pottering about.

'You aren't referring to Dad, are you?'

'We've all got our handicaps. Your father isn't the easiest of people to get on with. Like all people with strong enthusiasms he can be very selfish.'

'Do you think he realises it or not?'

'He does and he doesn't, I imagine. If you take his enthusiasm away what are you left with?'

'You tell me Mum.'

'You are left with a petulant man, and that's worse.'

'That sounds like blackmail, emotional blackmail.'

'It isn't conscious or deliberate. It just happens. If people have strong convictions or interests you can't suppress them, that way lies trouble.'

'Trouble and strife for the trouble and strife.'

'That's it. So they have to be diverted, re-chanelled a bit. That's the only way.'

'Well you can't re-channel deafness. Now we're back to where we started.' Fiona got up and joined her mother at the window.

'There's a difference between those handicaps which happen after you're married, which you share together, perhaps watch together with horror when they come, and those which were there before you started together. I think those are harder to put up with, those already in position. You must think carefully before you let your friendship with Jules develop.'

'Yes, I must Mum. Thanks for the tip.'

6

Jules could feel a cloud of despair forming as he travelled back in the bus. He could almost sense it gathering round him, swirling gently and yet with a menace he could not pinpoint. He thought of the Love Song of J. Alfred Prufrock: 'The yellow fog that rubs its back upon the window panes, the yellow smoke that rubs its muzzle on the window panes, licked its tongue into the corners of the evening.'

It wasn't so much licking its tongue, more salivating; Jules shuddered as he felt the cold damp droplets brush softly over him. Any minute now and they would be inside, spreading their dankness all through his being, snuffing out his spark.

He looked round the bus with alarm. The other passengers were oblivious of his predicament. They stared complacently out of the windows and digested their food and their lives in composure. Jules envied them.

When he arrived home he paused at the foot of the stairs. He could not decide whether to go to his room or to seek out his parents. He was standing there when Mary, hearing the front door open and close, came into the hall from the kitchen, wiping her hands on a towel.

'Oh. There you are Jules. Have a nice time?'

She had come in front of him so that he could see her lips. This annoyed Jules, who frowned and made no reply.

'What's the matter?' Mary gazed earnestly into his face and smiled.

She extended a hand to grasp his arm. Jules stood immobile, riven with his feelings, unable to respond.

43

'Don't you hear me Jules? You must hear me. You're not that deaf. Come on now, please Jules. What on earth's the matter?'

Jules stood still. It was as if the turmoil of his feelings took all his energy, all his willpower, leaving him a hulk. A hulk burning at the centre. Soon I shall be consumed, he thought. What matter? Still he stood.

Mary released her grip on his arm. She wondered what to do and heard the rustle of Peter folding his paper in the sitting-room and went in.

'Peter, didn't you hear all that? For goodness sake, come and help. I don't know what's got into Jules here. He won't do anything. He's just standing there in the hall.'

'I heard something going on.' Peter stood up and smiled to reassure Mary. 'I'm sure there must be some explanation. Perhaps he's playing some game. To see how long he can keep up this silence, or something like that.'

In the hall Jules had not budged.

'Come on old chap.' Peter went towards him, putting his hand forward. 'Drop this game now.' He shook Jules gently by grasping his arm.

Suddenly Jules exploded. 'Leave me alone!' he shouted.

Peter stood back, startled by the sudden outburst. Jules turned abruptly on his heel and walked down to the hall window and stared out, his hands clasped behind his back. He remained in that position for some time. Mary and Peter looked at each other in amazement. They had never seen Jules behave like this and were nonplussed.

'What's got into the boy?' Peter said to Mary.

'I rather feel it's all been a bit too much for him, the last few days. I suspect something went wrong with his visit to Fiona and her family and that has been the final straw. I think we had better leave him for a bit.'

'We are just going into the sitting-room,' she said to Jules, peering round so that he could see her lips.

Jules made no response and Peter and Mary sat uneasily, uncertain what to do.

Jules felt an impulse building up in him to fling open the

front door and go outside, and yet at the same time he seemed locked into his present position. He felt unable to make any decision and heard himself groaning out, 'Oh no!'

'What was that?' asked Mary. 'Should we go to him, do you think?'

She stood up and started to walk towards the door. Then she stopped and looked back at Peter.

'He might do something stupid,' she added.

'We had best leave him be.'

Presently they heard Jules mount the stairs. They did not hear his bedroom door and wondered where he was.

After a little while Mary said 'I can't stand it any longer. I'm going up, now.'

'Right, I'll come too.'

All was quiet upstairs.

'I wonder if he's locked his door?'

'I don't think there's a key,' Mary said. 'Shall we try it?'

Peter carefully turned the handle and gently opened the door. Jules was lying on his bed, on his back, staring at the ceiling. He turned soulful eyes towards his parents. His expression conveyed such desolation that Mary ran forward and hugged him to her.

'Jules. My darling.' She clung to him. Peter sat on the edge of the bed.

Jules's breathing became deeper and deeper until it broke into heaves and then subsided. Tears started to trickle down his cheeks. They stained Mary's blouse.

'Hey, look what you're doing you silly old thing.' Mary laughed. Jules grinned sheepishly.

Peter spotted Jules's school first eleven cricket cap hung on the side of the dressing table mirror. He went over to get it.

'Look Jules. Do you remember when you failed to get into the first team one year? How disappointed you were? It was a different story the next year.' Peter put the cap on his head and grinned cheekily.

Jules suddenly felt something unlock inside him at the sight of his father with the cap on, evoking memories of his childhood.

'You look ridiculous, Dad. I know you're trying to cheer me

45

up but my deafness is incurable. I am stuck with it for the rest of my life. The rest of my life, think of that.'

'People have overcome worse handicaps than that. It's all from within. It's got to come from within.'

'I know, Dad, but there's nothing within to come out.'

'There will be, you mark my words. Hang on and see.'

They all remained seated on the bed for a while.

'We must look like I don't know what, perched here.' Mary wiped a small tear from her eye with a brush of her hand. 'Let's go down . . .'

'For a nice cup of tea,' Peter and Jules intoned simultaneously.

'How did you guess?'

'We thought you were never going to ask.'

Jules felt better as they were drinking the tea, and related the day's events to Peter and Mary.

'I can see why you felt pretty chuckered,' Peter commented at the end. 'We men have to put up with a lot of anguish over women. They're rather basic people really. They claim to be more sensitive and emotional but I'm not so sure. I don't think they suffer like we do, how say you Jules?'

Jules paused. 'I expect you're right Dad.'

Peter went on, 'Under our rugged exterior there lies a sensitive soul. A chrysalis of compassion waiting to be encouraged.'

'Well, I think it's time we all pupated for the night.' Mary stood up and cleared the cups.

☆　☆　☆

Jules struggled through the weeks ahead and learnt to manage without his usual zest, welcoming it when it made momentary appearances.

Assignations for concerts came in as before. His Sunday stints at St Swain's Church in Mayfair occasioned him most grieving but he persevered. Fiona always greeted him with overt friendliness but a shadow would come over her welcome if he suggested any outing. Even the offer of a cup of coffee together after the rehearsal would meet with a hesitant prevarication, Jules noticed.

On the other hand, there seemed an increasing awareness between Boris and Fiona of each other's presence. Little glances of intimacy when something occurred to amuse them or someone made a remark which interested or intrigued them. The strands of familiarity were gradually binding them. Jules's initial aspiration to weaken or dissolve these ties faded with time and was replaced with bitterness which spilled over one evening.

Jules was lingering in the porch of the church after rehearsals, partly from a general lassitude and partly from a still-flickering hope that Fiona would agree to going out with him that evening. He heard voices coming from the body of the church and saw Fiona and Boris emerge. They had their outdoor coats on and were laughing together. Boris had his arm round Fiona's waist. To Jules he appeared to be gloating when he saw Jules.

'Hello Jules. Did you enjoy the practice? I thought it went well tonight. Didn't you Fiona?'

Fiona nodded and looked across at Jules. Jules thought he detected a momentary look of softness, even of compassion, in her glance.

'It was pretty good,' Jules responded. 'I've known better.'

'It takes a lot to please you, then. Perhaps your hearing is a handicap. I wonder how long you will be able to manage?'

Boris had not intended to say anything hurtful to Jules. He was genuinely sorry for him, but when rivalry over a girlfriend is at stake the niceties of feeling are apt to go by the board. The turkey cock struts and crows and will not be denied.

'I manage perfectly well, thank you. I can hear your snide remarks, anyway. Not that they're worth hearing.' Jules gave a bitter laugh.

Fiona watched with mounting sadness. 'Come on boys, lets all go for a coffee.'

She felt Boris tighten his grip round her waist and fancied he gave her a little pinch. She frowned.

'Come on then,' Boris said suddenly. 'Are you coming Jules, or are you buzzing off?'

47

Jules had been undecided until that remark. 'Yes, I'm coming all right.'

They went to their usual café and found a table. Jules realised that the background noise of chatter and clatter made his hearing even worse than usual and he could only manage to follow the drift of conversation if he stared intently at his companions' lips. This he found embarrassing and he felt his face flushing up and his irritability with it.

'You're finding it difficult to hear, aren't you Jules? We'll speak up a bit.'

'There's really no need.'

'You want to hear what we're saying, don't you?' Boris thrust his face close to Jules's and exaggerated his lip movements.

To Jules, Boris seemed to be mocking him rather as a normal person might address an imbecile, or a foreigner who cannot speak English.

'I wish to hear what you are saying when you have something useful to say.'

Jules turned to Fiona. 'Is he always like this?'

Fiona looked alarmed. The last thing she wanted was to get embroiled in this petty quarrel. Although I suppose it's not so petty really, she thought.

'Now stop it, both of you. You're just aggravating each other.'

'I'm only trying to help.' Jules wagged his head, aping Boris. 'You could best help by clearing off, that's all.'

'What? And leave you with Fiona? She doesn't want to be left with a cripple.'

Fiona stood up. She looked furious. 'I'm off. I'm certainly not staying here to listen to you two argue.'

She stalked out, her cup of coffee steaming morosely at her place at the table.

'Look what you've done now,' Boris almost shouted. 'You and your silly handicap. It would be better if people acknowledged their defects and acted accordingly.'

'What do you mean by that, Boris Striman? I suppose you think all people with handicaps, as you so call it, should withdraw gracefully, clutching our begging bowls, and leave the field open to you. You perfect specimens; I seem to have heard all that before. The Aryan race. Shall I stand up and give you the Nazi salute?'

'I dare you,' Boris snarled.

'You think I wouldn't, you smart aleck. You just see.'

Jules stood up, clicked his heels and raised his right arm stiffly, 'Heil Boris.'

The customers around stared in amazement and one or two laughed openly.

Someone called out, 'Where's your moustache then, Adolf?'

Jules did not hear him. He sat down and wondered why everyone was laughing at him.

'What's so funny?' he asked Boris.

'For God's sake, shut up.'

Jules was too overwrought to be able to comply. 'I should have realised that those with handicaps not only have to put up with the handicap but are an object for ridicule as well. Talk about rubbing salt into the wound. But it's the way of life I suppose. The fit must survive and breed. That's the way the race advances. And look where it's got us,' Jules added bitterly. 'I see the mate has gone to her nest to await the victor. Typical female reaction.'

By now Boris's feelings were jangling round inside him in an inchoate medley, rather like those toy kaleidoscopes with pieces of multicoloured glass which form different patterns with every twist. He gazed irresolute and increasingly despondent.

'I see my presence inspires all the bad emotions in people. I'd better leave.'

7

Jules's apprehension that his deafness might handicap or even end his musical career proved unfounded.

His letter in *The Times* drew forth a protracted correspondence on the subject of music and deafness from which Jules's career emerged not only unscathed but even fortified. Letters rained in to the paper from music therapists, from deaf musicians presenting a wide range of instrumental accomplishments in spite of their disability and from a host of other people who's lives had been enriched by music. In the end the paper declared the correspondence would be closed, there seeming to be no end to the flood of letters on the subject.

On a groundswell of renewed contentment and confidence Jules sailed through the days like a ship before the wind.

Jules had whetted Fletcher's appetite for furthering his nature studies when he had described his visit to Gilbert's house close by Epping Forest.

'You simply must arrange a get-together,' he told Jules sternly and his eagerness was such that Jules found himself escorting Fletcher to the Blake household one fine Saturday.

He wondered whether Fiona would be out and, if she were in, whether she would wish to see him.

They arrived mid-morning and were greeted by Gilbert and Marigold. It was a fine early summer's day so Gilbert was clad in a check shirt, open at the neck, and khaki shorts. His broad features were smiling and his blue eyes twinkled above a short bristly moustache. Jules and Fletcher, as befitted visitors unsure of exactly what awaited them, were more soberly clad in flannels and cardigans over shirts.

Coffee was served in the garden. Fletcher glanced round approvingly at the scene.

'A nice set-up you've got here Gilbert. I envy you.'

Gilbert smiled with satisfaction. 'Chosen carefully. Chosen very carefully, Fletcher.'

'Have you always been interested in nature study?'

'I'll say so. Can't get it out of my system.'

'That's true enough,' Marigold laughed. 'I think he only married me for my name.'

'Are you familiar with the writings of Rudolph Otto? He was a German Protestant theologian. He died in 1937?'

'If you're going to quote him,' Marigold said laughing, 'I'm off.'

As she left she turned towards Fletcher. 'Don't let him go on about Rudolph Otto too long or you'll regret it.'

Gilbert grinned at Fletcher and Jules. 'Just a sentence or two, nothing more. It's so apt, you've got to hear it.'

The other two sat quietly as Gilbert looked up to the sky and recalled the phrases:

' "Nature-mysticism is the sense of being immersed in the oneness of nature . . . He who is dances with the motes of dust and radiates with the sun. He rises with the dawn, surges with the wave, is fragrant in the rose, rapt with the nightingale." '

'I'm afraid it's a bit of a mouthful, but he puts it well, don't you think?'

'Very well.' Fletcher pondered. 'Talking of the nightingale, did Jules tell you about our efforts to influence the bird-song?'

Jules, who had been watching carefully, shook his head. Fletcher related what had happened.

'I've been reading Gilbert White since. I expect you are very familiar with him.'

'Oh yes.'

'Do you remember his observations on owls, for instance?'

'I haven't read him recently.'

'He got a friend to ascertain the pitch of the owl's hoot with a pitch pipe and it was found to be B flat, mostly, anyway. The nightingale's song was too flowing, too liquid to pinpoint in the same way. Cuckoos were mostly D. He also refers to the snoring of owls.'

Gilbert looked excited. 'Yes, I've heard that,' he said. 'In fact I had two aunts who lived in the country. They had an outhouse near their bedrooms, one of their bedrooms anyway, and one night this aunt was terrified at this snoring she heard. She thought there was a man asleep somewhere on the premises. She got her sister and they both heard it. They didn't sleep a wink all night and were too frightened to go to investigate.

The snoring had stopped by the morning and of course they found nothing. I was summoned and spent several nights there to no avail. But one evening later I got a phone call from them to say the snoring was there again. I didn't live far away so I hurried over and, sure enough, I heard this snoring. When I went out to investigate, the snoring suddenly stopped – and I saw an owl fly out from an open window in the shed! We had a good laugh about that one. They heard him a few times after that. Sometimes he screeched; when he had a mouse, I suppose.'

Fletcher looked excited. 'That's very interesting, because I've heard owls screeching where we live and I think they come from the boilerhouse next to our church. I would love to investigate and record those owls snoring or whatever noises they choose to make, day or night.'

'You would think they would snore during the day, knowing their nocturnal habits. I would love to come over and help in any way I can.' Gilbert gleamed with anticipation.

'Right, then. That's on. Are you game, Jules?'

Jules smiled. 'Not the church again. Oh well, I suppose you can count me in.'

'In for a screech, in for a snore, I promise you this, it won't be a bore.' Fletcher laughed and rubbed his hands with glee.

'Well come on Fletcher. I had better show you round my domain now you're here. Are you coming, Jules?'

'I'll sit here and contemplate the pleasures in store, patrolling the churchyard in the silvery light of the moon, where we used to kiss and swoon.'

'So that's where you did it,' exclaimed Fletcher,
' "So smooth, so sweet, so silvery is thy voice,
As, could they hear, the damned would make no noise,
But listen to thee (walking in they chamber)
Melting melodious words to lutes of amber." '
'Not very appropriate,' Fletcher retorted. 'I shouldn't think the damned would make any noise in the churchyard. Hardly the place.'

Just then Jules espied Fiona looking out from the kitchen window. She made no sign of recognition but stared as if undecided what to do. A thrill went through him, followed rapidly by a despondency, followed in its wake by a flood of memories. It was if the despondency were marching ahead waving a banner warning off any bright spirits which might be about, rather as a man waving a red warning flag preceded the prototype motor cars in Edwardian times.

Jules took a deep breath and sat there. Fiona withdrew from the window and turned round. Marigold was watching her.

'You're wondering what to do, aren't you? Whether to go out to Jules or not?'

Fiona sighed. 'That's it Mum. That's just it.'

She shook her head sadly and walked across the kitchen floor, as if to leave.

'Well, are you fond of him or not?'

'I suppose I don't know. At times I feel I am fond of him, perhaps even love him, but at other times I don't feel like that. I can't sort it out.'

'You must be careful not to let pity influence your feelings too much. I don't think pity would be a solid foundation for a relationship. Most sieve-like.'

'What on earth do you mean Mother, most sieve-like?'

'I don't know. Not very watertight, I suppose.'

'In fact I think I'll see Jules. I've made up my mind.'

'That only goes to show how contingent are our decisions. Are they carefully thought out? Not on your nelly. Off you go then. Tell them lunch won't be long.'

Fiona went into the garden and came up to where Jules was sitting, apparently lost in his thoughts. He did not hear her

54

approach and was startled when she touched him lightly on the shoulder.

'Goodness, you gave me a fright.' He stood up.

'Let's go for a stroll. There's just time before lunch, Mum says.'

When they were clear of the house she took hold of Jules's arm and peered into his face so that he could see her lips.

'I'm sorry I stalked out the other night from the café.' She paused and smiled. They walked on in silence.

'I don't know what to say. You'd every right to. I don't blame you. I am going deaf and I've got to face up to it. I suppose if Beethoven and Bizet could put up with it I shall have to.'

'I don't think you can say that Beethoven did put up with it, not really. He behaved abominably at times, I believe, and Bizet had cracked his music open by the time he was.'

'So it's different for me, is it? I've never started and so have no excuse to behave abominably, is that it?' Jules sounded bitter.

'I didn't mean it like that. I didn't mean to upset you. Oh dear.'

Fiona felt her good and warm feelings slipping away. Like through that sieve mother mentioned; perhaps she was right, Fiona thought.

They trudged on gloomily. Jules kicked a stone in his path violently into the hedge.

Fiona's glumness deepened. 'Did you have to do that?'

Jules glowered ahead and turned round abruptly. 'Let's go back.'

They exchanged no further words.

Marigold had set out lunch in the sun room overlooking the back of the garden. The soup was steaming on the hob and a large crusty loaf lay on the table with its escort, the bread knife, like an ocean liner and a submarine ready to plunder it.

'Call the men in will you, Fiona?'

Fiona was glad to escape to the garden. She found her father and Fletcher apparently contemplating a yellow duster hanging on the line.

'Haven't you got anything more interesting to do than stare at that yellow duster, for goodness sake? Lunch is ready.'

'Have you noticed something about it, young lass?' Gilbert said.

Fiona looked at the duster with a slight tilt of her head away from it, as if to say, 'It's not really worthy of my attention but I had better show willing.'

'What's so wonderful about it? I can see a few smudges on it.'

'Ah. But there's something else. Come closer.'

Now Fiona could see that a whole mass of small flies had congregated on it. A blue duster nearby was bereft of insects.

'Yellow is the flavour of the month, or at least the colour of the month,' Fletcher added helpfully. 'Yellow flowers are in at the moment, so insects go for that colour selectively.'

'Well you two won't be flavour of the month if you don't come in to lunch. It's soup to start. If it's yellow soup all the flies will get there first, unless you're quick,' she added helpfully.

'All right. You'll do.'

They all settled down round the table with that little touch of confraternity which develops among people about to enjoy food together. The soup steamed from the huge china ladle which Marigold wielded and the crusty loaf crackled as it was sliced and bitten into.

Jules, because of his deafness, felt his crunching as he chewed even more clearly than the rest, unburdened as his ear was with outside distractions. His mood mellowed and he smiled across at Fiona. She noticed his satisfaction and responded to the glow of pleasure which lighted up his face. When she looked round she found all their faces showed a similar mood. She smiled and bit deeply into her crust. A shower of crumbs fell from her mouth and peppered her soup. They all laughed.

'That's my girl,' Gilbert exclaimed. 'Bite while you can. While your teeth are firm and stout. Make them work for their living.'

'You've certainly done that for yours,' Marigold laughed.

'You've not done so badly yourself,' Gilbert retorted. 'Talk about the pot calling the kettle black.'

'That reminds me –' Marigold went to fill the kettle.

'Which day are you coming over, then?' Fletcher enquired as they drank their tea.

'How about Saturday?'

'Right. Next Saturday. If you like you'd better stay overnight in case we have to wait for the snoring. I hope they come up to screech now we want them to.'

Jules suddenly had a thought. He beckoned Fiona aside.

'Fiona, I've got a bright idea. It would be a pity to disappoint them, don't you think?'

Fiona gave him a quizzical look. 'Are you thinking what I'm thinking you're thinking?'

'I think I am thinking what you think I am thinking.'

They both burst out laughing.

'What are you two up to?' Marigold asked.

'No good, I'll be bound,' Gilbert added. Jules and Fiona drew further away.

'Will you come over with your dad, Fiona? And practice your owl snoring in the meantime.'

'Shall I add a few hoots to the repertoire while I'm about it?'

'Sure. But discreetly. Sotto-owlish, if you know what I mean.'

'B flat it is then.'

'And in the meantime be natural.' He winked.

8

The following Saturday morning Gilbert was up bright and early. He bustled about getting things ready.

'What shall I wear, Marigold?'

Marigold raised a sleepy head from the pillow. 'Well, we're staying overnight and as it's Sunday tomorrow you'd better go in something respectable. I should wear your grey flannels and a shirt and blazer. Take an old cardigan you can put on while you're owling. You had better see if Fiona's on the go. I haven't heard her yet. I've arranged for Aunt Mabel to stay with the boys.'

Gilbert rattled at Fiona's door and then opened it. 'Come on girl, get cracking. We're off to the Pembertons' today in case you had forgotten. Do you want any breakfast?'

'Just get me a nice cup of tea please, Dad.' She turned over and stretched out her arms. 'What's it like?'

'Lovely. Get going before you miss the best part of the day.' He called the boys.

Gilbert loved the mornings. They were his best times. He enjoyed hearing the familiar morning noises: the whine of the milkman's van followed by the crunch of his feet on the gravel, the birds of course, with their chirrups and flutings, the sound of his boiler starting its duties for the day, the chink of light between the curtains from which he tried to guess what the weather was like.

When he went out of doors everything became more vivid and the cool air shot him with a bolt of its vigour.

'You're far too hearty in the mornings,' Marigold would

admonish him – and then give him a friendly peck, or just a shove in his side.

He would grin and go to put on the kettle.

In due course Fiona appeared, wearing slacks of pale blue and a yellow jumper.

'Goodness gracious, that'll send the insects wild.'

'I wonder if the owls will notice.'

'Might stop them snoring. Short gasps of owlish breaths more likely.'

'Seriously, Dad, will it be all right? I don't want to spoil your fun.'

'They can always look the other way. Have you noticed how they seem to be able to turn their heads through 360 degrees?'

'Very useful attribute. Must have remarkable survival value. Just think what an advantage it must be to be able to turn your head through a whole circle in the forest. I should think an oak tree might look a bit different when viewed from eyes which have just circumnavigated the circumference of a circle. Must do wonders for the blood supply throbbing away in the poor creature's head. Positively apoplectic.'

'You're in a rather strange mood today, my girl. I hope you behave yourself.'

'Why do you think I've got these slacks on? If we're shinning up and down ladders for instance.'

'It had crossed my mind that you thought your profile displayed itself in a rather comely manner in that particular garment.'

Marigold appeared in the kitchen. 'What on earth are you two chattering on about? I see very little sign of progress as regards the breakfast.'

'Well, Fiona said she would make do with a cup of tea.'

'No. She won't make do with a cup of tea. You both ought to have more than that. I'll do you some toast. And we'll make enough for the boys too.'

After breakfast they set off. Fletcher and Doris were waiting for them when they arrived.

'I think we had better go round and ask the vicar if we may investigate his owls,' Fletcher suggested when they had settled

60

in. 'We'll take the whole team. We can call and pick up Jules on the way.'

☆　☆　☆

The Reverend Ralph Dene was a bird-like forty-two. He was very tall with a slight stoop, which revealed the bald pate on top of his head. In contrast, dark hair flowed abundantly from the sides and denied all attempts, which Ralph had now largely abandoned, at regimentation. He was given to sudden movements when the hair would bound about as if sharing the air of excitement which generally seemed to accompany him.

Winifred his wife was a year older and had a habit of gazing over things as if in a sudden fit of abstraction.

She had probably anticipated further growth from Ralph and had not wanted to be caught napping, Fletcher had joked to Doris.

Winifred admitted them into the rectory and Ralph emerged from his study.

'Ah. A deputation,' he exclaimed with manifest delight. 'Do come in.'

The four were rapidly propelled into the study and introductions were made.

'Ralph, you know you've got owls in your boilerhouse – and possibly in the church too, I've mentioned it before. We wish to study them.'

'So you have, so you have. Bats in the belfry, that's what they say. Call me that sometimes, I expect I am really.'

'Well, you said it,' Winifred laughed and inspected the ceiling. 'I don't know how I put up with him, Fletcher, what say you?'

'You'd miss the old monster if he weren't about.'

Then Fletcher heard the words he had been dreading.

'I shall join in the escapade.' Ralph stood up decisively. 'I shall lend a hand.'

'That's only because it gets you out of writing your sermon.'

'I shall draw moral precepts from our harmless little endeavours.'

'I only hope they are harmless,' Fletcher muttered to Gilbert.

61

'There's an element of Michael Crawford or Frank Spencer about our Ralph I'm afraid.'

'We wish,' Fletcher assumed a heavy, sonorous delivery to impress the importance of the matter on to Ralph, 'to make a record of the owls snoring. That is our prime target.'

Ralph burst out laughing and clapped his hands with delight. 'You can't be serious. Not really. How old are you Fletch? Perhaps you're over the top.'

He paused, suddenly aware that Fletcher's companions would feel themselves included in his strictures. His hand covered his mouth with horror.

'I'm sorry, I didn't mean to be rude. I was just stunned.'

'Better if you had been,' Winifred said wryly.

A notion struck Ralph. 'Perhaps it's the owls I hear during my sermons. Of course it is. My congregation would not dream of doing such a thing.'

'They would just dream, I expect.'

Ralph frowned at Fletcher's remark and then slapped him jocularly.

'You old devil. I didn't see you at church last Sunday. One of my best sermons too, though I say it myself. But enough of banter. Where shall we canter?'

'Oh Lord,' Fletcher sighed. 'Give him a bromide someone.'

'No fear,' retorted Winifred, 'I want him thoroughly tired out so that I can get some peace at night.'

'Don't worry, Winifred. We may have to do some of the recording tonight if we make no progress during the day.'

The five investigators set off for the church. As they neared the boilerhouse, a red brick building next to the church, Fletcher placed his forefinger to his lips.

'SSSShhhh.'

They dumped their equipment inside the church porch and tiptoed round the side. Mrs Doherty, passing by, gazed in amazement as she saw the vicar. He looked even taller and his stoop was enhanced by this manouevre, his side-curls floating up and down with his exaggerated motion. He looked for all the world like a huge ibis, without a beak, accompanied by his flock. A motley crew, Mrs Doherty thought.

'Are you beating the bounds, vicar?' She shouted across.

This comment produced a remarkable result. The vicar detached himself from the group and came arrowing towards her at an alarming rate. Mrs Doherty drew back. For a long time she had viewed him with a certain misgiving.

'I wonder where eccentricity ends and madness begins', she had observed enigmatically to Mr Doherty one day.

Not knowing to whom this remark referred, her husband gave a guarded reply. 'Might overlap shouldn't wonder.' He left it at that.

The vicar arrived, panting. 'Mrs Doherty, I must beseech you to silence. We are engaged on a most particular investigation for which silence is required, nay essential.'

'Well you had better tell it to the pilot of that plane going over, Vicar.'

'Those regular noises don't matter, Mrs Doherty.'

He returned to the others. Mrs Doherty watched them tiptoe to the door of the boilerhouse.

Then she was astonished to see the vicar desert his flock and streak back to the vicarage with what she could only think of as a tiptoe sprint. I wonder if they have thought of that as a category for the next Olympics, she mused, but resisted the temptation to hail him when she saw him returning with the boilerhouse key.

Ralph mutely handed the key to Fletcher, his breath being in short supply for the moment. Fletcher tried to turn the key. It resisted and gave out a mild squeak of protest. He paused.

'Oh Lord.' Ralph took a gulp of air and shot off again.

'Where on earth is he off to now?' Gilbert asked.

They shook their heads. Mrs Doherty stared with disbelief when she saw the vicar repeating his circuit, still on tiptoe.

He disappeared into the house and soon emerged, this time carrying an oilcan. The other four put their hands together in silent approbation. Ralph blew out his lips and cast his eyes to the heavens. Then he bent and directed a vigorous squirt of oil into the lock. He stood back and gestured to Fletcher with exaggerated politeness. This time the lock yielded and they tiptoed in.

A huge silvered boiler stood silently in the middle of the

space, sprouting tubes here and there which wandered their ways like demented serpents around the room and eventually to the outside. The silence was tinged with a smell of oil. Bird droppings adorned the floor at selected sites and traces of what seemed to be roasted droppings embellished the boiler at one end. Daylight could be discerned through the tiles and rafters. At one spot on the rafters two pairs of large eyes could be made out and then, as their eyes adapted to the dark, the whitish bodies of two barn owls.

All stood silent and still. The owls blinked at the intruders. Fletcher motioned his companions to go outside.

'Good. We've got 'em.'

'Yes, but they're not snoring.'

'I'll soon fix that,' Ralph whispered, 'I'll go and get my last sermon.' He pretended to dart off again.

'For goodness sake don't, Ralph,' Fletcher pleaded. 'I saw Mrs Doherty watching you and she'll have a fit if you dash off again.'

'How close do you think we can get?' Fiona whispered.

'The closer the better, I should imagine.' Ralph pointed excitedly to the top of the boiler. 'There,' he mouthed.

The others looked doubtful. They tiptoed out and went back to the church porch.

'I don't think "On top of Old Smokey" sounds terribly safe,' Gilbert said. 'The boiler might come on.'

'No. It won't do that. It's off for the summer.'

'Oh, where to?' Fiona laughed. 'Somewhere nice?'

'Nice and hot, where I'll send you, if you're not careful, young girl.' Ralph grinned at her.

Eventually they rigged up the recording apparatus on the ground, as near to the owls as possible.

'It's no use switching that thing on at the moment,' Fletcher observed. 'They might lie doggo for aeons. One of us will just have to stay here on duty and switch on when the owls stir. What say you all?'

A rota was agreed and Fletcher took the first stand. He waited patiently but no snoring was to be heard either from the owls or from their watcher.

64

By early evening Fiona and Jules took their turn, together because of Jules's deafness and company for Fiona. While they were seated on two rickety old chairs Ralph had produced, Fiona's hand suddenly grabbed Jules's arm.

'Look.'

The owls were stretching their necks and showing signs of animation. They flurried their feathers and gurgled in a brooding sort of way. All at once they took wing and noiselessly exited through a gap in the juncture of the roof and side wall.

'They've gone,' Jules exclaimed. 'Did we miss anything? There was no time to switch on.'

'If we missed anything, then it escaped me,' Fiona responded. 'Now's our chance to do what we planned.'

'Right.'

They switched on the apparatus and stood back from the microphone. Jules signalled with his hand, 'Now'.

They began to snore owlishly, with pauses dictated by their almost overwhelming inclination to giggle from time to time, especially when Jules gave a particularly impressive snore followed by a throaty gurgle.

When they were running out of permutations on the basic snore, Fiona emitted a piercing screech and they both stopped and switched off. They collapsed onto each other with merriment and gasped for breath between their laughs.

'If only the owls would return while we are still here and make a bit of a noise, it would add authenticity to our efforts, don't you think, Jules?'

'Yes. If only.'

They huddled hopefully and presently they heard a fluttering and spotted the owls returning to their perches, each with something held in the beak. Jules darted and switched on just in time to catch first one owl and then the other let out a horrendous screech before pecking at their morsels.

'That shows they can talk with their mouths full,' Jules laughed. 'Probably the height of good manners in owl society. The top echelons, anyhow. I'm sure Ralph would only entertain the top.'

Soon Gilbert appeared at the door.

'What's the news? I detect a sense of quiet satisfaction. Have you had any luck?'

'Yes we have,' Jules said. 'First of all we got them snoring, then they went off to hunt and came back and screeched for us. It's all there on tape.'

'Capital,' said Gilbert,

'No, His Master's Voice. At least His Feathered Eminence's Voice,' Fiona chipped in.

'We had better go back and see if Fletcher wants any more.'

On the strength of Jules's and Fiona's story it was decided to pack up the equipment for the day and play it back at the Pembertons'.

Doris prepared coffee and they all sat round with bated breath while Fletcher set up his apparatus. Doris watched with a smile on her face.

'Nothing he likes better than fiddling with his bits and pieces. It doesn't matter what they say, it's the setting up he likes, I think.'

'Bit like a keen gardener,' Marigold observed. 'They're always planning the next thing and never seem to have time to enjoy the present thing.'

'Oh, that's unjust!' Gilbert exclaimed.

'I'm not so sure, I rather agree with Mum.'

Fletcher straightened up from his labours.

'Now then everybody. All ears please. Lend me your ears.'

He threw the switch. The loudspeaker emitted the signs of animation which loudspeakers usually give when heralding a performance, in the form of a low background buzz overlaid with staccato squeaks and whistles. Suddenly a new sound was heard, a mixture of snoring and snorting.

Fletcher looked enraptured. 'Shush. That's it. Listen now!'

The more they listened the more doubt arose in their minds. There was a break in the sound followed by a faint undulant sort of noise and then two or three piercing screeches of such a manifest and genuine owl-like nature as strongly to reinforce the rising doubts over the snoring. There was a click as it ended.

Fiona and Jules found it necessary to frown in order to mask their merriment, which was trying to surface like an air balloon held underwater by a flimsy piece of string.

'That last bit quite startled me,' Gilbert said at last. 'I didn't know what to make of the first part, the snoring. Sounded rum to me.'

'Me too,' said Doris. 'I should know, being an expert on such matters.'

'What do you mean, dear?' Fletcher pretended a look of innocent bewilderment.

'You two didn't fall asleep by any chance, did you?' Marigold looked at Fiona and Jules. 'I thought I recognised the sounds a bit, reminded me of someone who shall be nameless before her tonsils came out.'

Fiona could keep it back no longer. She burst out laughing and Jules soon followed suit. The others joined in.

'So that's it. They've spoofed it. Hook, line and tonsil, from the sound of it. Thus goes scientific endeavour, invalidated by pranksters.'

Directly he had said this Fletcher felt he had been too severe.

'You two can jolly well pay a forfeit for this. I propose to the assembly that we vote on whether the two culprits shall spend the remainder of the night incarcerated in the boilerhouse to make a true and genuine recording of the night owls.'

The voting was unanimous in favour, with two abstentions.

'Might I suggest a compromise,' Fiona volunteered, 'if we get a genuine recording from the owls can we then pack it in?'

'Agreed.'

They were lucky and three hours later were able to conclude their task with honour restored.

9

Boris Striman felt perplexed and unhappy. The acid in him worked on his features as on a etching, burrowing into the grooves and deepening them. His normal expression of intent alertness was moulded into one of grim resolve, untinged with any of the softer virtues.

He strove to perfect his piano playing but the relish had gone. He wondered why. His thoughts continually turned to Jules. They had known each other since schooldays, and he suspected that his malaise was not unconnected with his relationship with his friend. A love, born of a long-continued association and the ups and downs inherent in such a sustained friendship, was fighting a battle with newer feelings of rivalry and jealousy. He was the battlefield. At times he could almost watch the antagonists flexing their sinews and polishing their armour somewhere in his soul but at other times one or the other took over and involved him in the conflict.

He was only too aware of Jules's deafness and now found it unbelievable that he could have stooped so low as to perpetrate such a deceit on his friend.

He contemplated what the effects of his tampering with the piano in the Wigmore Hall must have had, and were still having no doubt, on Jules. He had started a train of events he was now powerless to arrest. Somehow when he was younger he always felt faults could be rectified but now he envisaged his one act of betrayal as a monster ninepin which he had deliberately pushed over and was now causing a ripple effect down lanes of ninepins which stretched beyond the horizon, many of them looking like Jules with a rather startled expression on his face, his eyes starting with amazement and later with horror and despair. The fact that Jules had assured him his career was going fine did not seem to register with Boris.

He wondered whether he would feel better if he owned up to Jules. What would Jules do and say? Would it do any good or merely upset him more? Then there was Fiona. What would she make of it all? A confession would certainly finish any hope in that direction.

All these thoughts were going through Boris's mind as he sat in his place in St Swain's Church one Sunday. Jules was two places down the line of choristers and Fiona was opposite. Her cheeks were rosy today and her green eyes glanced more at Jules than in his direction Boris noted with a pang.

After the practice was over he found himself in front of Fiona possessed only with the thought that he must regain her approbation and admiration.

'Fiona. Let's go off for a snack somewhere. I haven't seen you for ages.'

He noticed her eyes momentarily veil and knew he would have to fight for what he craved.

'Oh come on. I've lots to tell you.'

'And I've lots to tell you.'

'Well it's snap then, isn't it? Come on.' He took her arm and urged her forward to the door.

She glanced round. Jules was in the background and saw her look. He gave a fleeting smile which seemed to turn into a query but made no motion. Fiona felt a surge of exasperation. If he could not show more fight than that, what did he deserve? She paused irresolute.

'Come on,' Boris urged. He sensed the situation. Fiona stepped out.

They found a small café and ordered sandwiches and coffee.

Boris felt great. 'Who's going to relate first. Who's bursting the most.'

'You go on,' Fiona laughed. 'I can tell you're dying to tell me all, or nearly all. I'll never get a hearing until you've done.'

'Well, I've been practising hard, especially a rather difficult piece by Chopin and, would you believe it, I've been engaged to recite it in Sheffield.'

'That's wonderful.' Fiona leant forward and patted his arm. Then she gave it a squeeze.

Boris felt elated. 'How about coming with me? What do you say. It's on Wednesday, the twentieth of next month. Surely you can get a day off. Do come.'

Fiona felt like responding there and then but hesitated. 'I'll have to see.'

'You don't rule it out then? Great. Where there's a will there's a way, so they say.'

'Who's they?' Fiona laughed.

'They is them. All the others except us. Please manage it if you can.'

Just then Fiona spotted Jules outside the café. He appeared irresolute, standing peering in and then wandering away, only to return. He remained outside, arms by his side, glancing down at his feet. Boris noticed Fiona's attention was taken and glanced round.

'There's Jules.'

'So I see.' Boris did not sound enthusiastic. 'What on earth is he doing, standing around like a wet fish?'

'I imagine he is wondering whether to come in or not.'

'Well why doesn't he make up his mind? He's got a mind, I suppose?'

'That's hardly fair. I can imagine all sorts of thoughts tumbling through his mind right now and you know it.'

'Yes. I'm being unfair. He's got his problems, as we know. Shall I go and call him in?'

'Yes do.'

Boris went out to Jules. 'Hi Jules. We're in here. Coming to join us?'

Jules looked at Boris. His expression was troubled and he hesitated before it all poured out.

'The trouble is I don't know whether to try to be normal, behave as if I were normal, fight on on even terms you might say, or whether to give in and cease to struggle. Whether to say, "That, that and that are not for the likes of me. They're for the normal blokes not the handicapped ones", or whether to defy my handicap. But that way lies humiliation it seems to me.'

'Oh come on in and let's have a chat about it.' Boris more or less shoved Jules in through the door.

'Jules couldn't decide whether to come in or not so I shoved him in,' Boris told Fiona.

'Here under protest are we,' Fiona laughed.

Jules smiled. 'I don't know. I'm all in a muddle these days.'

'You've got to strike out for what you want,' Boris said with conviction.

'Yes, but if you want the wrong things, the impossible things, what then?' Jules looked puzzled. 'It's no good wanting the impossible things, or is it? I just don't know.'

'How do you know they're impossible unless you try?' Fiona asked.

'Well, there are some things which are clearly impossible. I couldn't win the heavyweight boxing title, for instance.'

'You could if you put lead weights in your gloves and got in the first blow.'

'You mean you can if you cheat.' Jules looked sharply at Boris. 'But if you cheat and win is that really a victory? Perhaps it's defeat.'

'That depends on the attitude of the victor I suppose,' Boris said slowly.

His thoughts ploughed deeply into his soul and emerged chastened. The allure of his Sheffield assignment, one which Jules might well have got had it not been for the Wigmore Hall episode, felt tarnished now in Boris's mind. He went very silent.

'What's come over you?' Fiona asked.

'I don't know.'

'Well something has, hasn't it?' Jules sounded more emphatic than he had done up till then. 'Is there something troubling you Boris, I wonder?'

Boris appeared to come to a decision. 'No. Nothing at all. I was just mulling over what we had been saying.'

'You disappoint me.'

'What on earth are you two on about? I don't follow the drift at all.' Fiona glanced from one to the other.

72

'We're getting too heavy. Let's talk about something else. I thought we sang well tonight, didn't you two?' Boris said.

A constraint fell amongst them and their chatter languished.

Presently Fiona excused herself. 'Well, I'm off. Got things to do before tomorrow. Bye bye boys.'

They stood up as she left and Jules prepared to leave himself. Boris drew him back down into his seat with almost a fierce shove.

'Hey Boris, what are you at? Careful now.'

'There's something I must tell you. I knew I must after our last few remarks just now.'

'What? About winning by cheating and all that?'

'Yes.' Boris's face registered intensity of feeling and he gave a dry swallow; his Adam's apple appearing to have difficulty in moving freely. 'You know about that time at The Wigmore Hall?'

'Of course I do.' Jules waited, sensing something important was coming.

'What would you say if I told you I had altered the tuning on that piano?'

There was a long pause. Jules's eyes bored into him.

'Did you really do that? I had my suspicions but couldn't really bring myself to believe you would do such a thing. How could you Boris?' Anger rose up in Jules like a magnesium flare and as soon faded.

Boris looked earnestly at him. 'I don't know what came over me. It seems now as if I was a different self. All I could think of was getting ahead of you by whatever means. I just can't think how I could feel like that now.' He gave a sardonic laugh.

'What's done is done and that's that. There's an end of it. Trouble is, it isn't an end of it, though. I've got to live with the consequences.' Jules laughed bitterly.

'I've learnt one thing,' Boris said with conviction. 'That is that you can pay too high a price for something.'

'What do you mean?'

'Well, ever since that time things have turned sour for me.' He paused reflectively. 'Perhaps now I've got it off my chest I'll feel better about it. I couldn't feel worse, anyway,' he added bitterly. 'Can you ever forgive me? I suppose not. It's too much to expect.'

'I don't know how I feel,' Jules replied. 'Rather stunned at the moment. I'll need time for it to sink in. It's one thing to suspect something and quite another to know it for sure.' Jules sighed. 'I feel just drained at the moment. Let's go home.'

'Who are you going to tell?' Boris asked anxiously.

'I hadn't thought of that. I dunno. What do you suggest?'

'I would much prefer no one else to know. Could we just keep it to ourselves?' Boris held Jules's arm. 'Or is that too much to ask?'

Jules took a deep breath. 'All right, I'll keep it to myself. Does that please you?'

'It is more than I deserve. I'll try to make it up to you, if I can.'

☆ ☆ ☆

A few days later Boris heard from Fiona that she would accompany him to Sheffield. His initial mood of rejoicing soon melted away to be replaced by one of exasperated perplexity.

Here he was, having promised Jules only a few days before that he would do all he could to help him, now in the position of whisking Fiona off to Sheffield. He could imagine Jules's reaction to that. Unlikely to be one of affable endorsement he thought wryly. He next pictured Fiona's response if he now told her he didn't want her to go with him. He envisaged her tossing her head, her dark curly hair flying in his face as it bounded contemptuously before him. Her green eyes would rake him with disdain. He could not face that. That was not what life was about. You had to fight for what you wanted; a craven approach was not for him. Let St Francis of Assisi do what he liked but Boris would stake his claim to life. Jules must fight his own battles.

They arranged to travel up by train and stay in student accommodation at the university.

'Does Jules know you're coming up to Sheffield?' Boris asked her.

'What's it got to do with him.' Fiona sounded aggrieved.

74

Jules had not contacted her since that time at the café. 'I just wondered.'

Jules had meanwhile been in his personal Garden of Gethsemane. The barometer of his self-esteem veered alarmingly from day to day, and even from hour to hour. Although his music was going well his perplexity over Fiona was undermining his confidence.

Peter and Mary watched and their hearts bled. They suffered with the poignant helplessness which only parents encounter.

'We must do something.' Mary slumped in a kitchen chair after washing up the breakfast things.

Peter was opening the mail. 'What can we do? We can't give him his hearing back and we can't make his decisions for him. We made him but now we can't make him. That just about sums it up.'

'Anything's better than this stalemate. It's Fiona more than the music I feel sure. We must talk to him again.'

'If you think it will do any good dear.'

'Well it can't be worse than the present situation.'

'Ah. Surely that's seeing it from your point of view, Mary. It may well be that anything is better than the present position from our point of view but what about his point of view. We could make it worse for him.'

'I don't see how. I really don't. We brought him up and guided him in the past. Why should we stop now?'

'Because he's older. More independent. Even so, I agree with you. I think we should try to talk to him and see how we get on.'

That evening Jules was sitting staring listlessly at the daily paper.

'Have you seen Boris or Fiona recently?' Mary enquired.

Jules stirred and frowned. After a long pause he said 'No.'

All three of them heard the clock ticking on the mantelshelf.

'Time moves on and decisions have to be made.' Peter said quietly.

'Sometimes it doesn't seem worth making decisions. They're

all made for you. The big ones anyway.'

'You can't let life walk over you. You mustn't,' Mary said.

'Why shouldn't I? What does it matter? If the most important things in life are denied then what do the rest matter? Trivia.' Jules snorted contemptuously.

'That just won't do lad and you know it.' Peter looked hard at Jules. 'Somewhere inside you there is a miniature emotional atomic bomb just waiting to be activated and galvanise you. It's a question of finding the key.'

'I might go up in smoke. Is that what you want Dad?'

'Anything would be better than inanition.'

'Oh Peter, how can you say such a thing?' Mary sounded exasperated but then she laughed. 'But I know what you mean. I think I do, anyway.'

'The way to do it is to get involved in something.'

'But I am Dad. My music.'

'No. I don't mean that. You can't see too clearly where that will lead. That's your problem. No, what you must do is get involved in something which is immediate, which has no long-term implications. Something which you know you can finish. Now what shall we think of?' Peter pondered.

'Something involving people,' Mary said. 'I always think that's best.'

'Typical woman's remark. But I think you're right. I think Ralph Dene is just the man.'

'What, our vicar?' Jules asked starting to look interested, 'he doesn't want to be bothered with me.'

'Yes, I'm sure he does. You've got the answer Peter. We'll ask him round.'

'No time like the present. It's not late. Strike while the iron's hot I say.'

'Before I have time to say no you mean,' Jules laughed. 'All right, go ahead and ask him.'

Ralph promised to be round when he had finished what he was doing and was as good as his word, appearing breezily in half-an-hour's time. They saw his tall, angular figure bustling down the drive, his gaze bent to his feet.

'Hello Ralph. Thanks for coming. We saw you coming up the

drive and thought you were in danger of walking right through the front door, you were inspecting your feet so assiduously.'

'Assiduously was it, dear Peter. I had a feeling that one of my feet didn't belong, it felt different from its companion. That's strange, isn't it? Hello Mary, hello Jules. Do my feet look all right to you two?'

'That's a strange question,' said Mary. 'Why do you ask?'

'Because they feel funny.'

They all scrutinised Ralph's feet. Suddenly Mary burst out laughing. 'You've got different shoes on. They don't match. One's got a patterned toe and the other hasn't.'

'Bless my soul, you're right Mary.'

'One of the blessed soles is wrong,' Jules said.

'It gives me an idea for my sermon next Sunday. Displaced souls being trodden underfoot and all that. Capital! Now, why did you want to see me?'

There was an awkward pause. Then Peter spoke up.

'Jules here is going through a bit of a bad patch, what with his deafness and one or two other things and we all thought that if he could get himself involved with something, take him out of himself as it were, it might help.'

Jules nodded. 'That's just it Ralph.'

'Of course I will help. I'd be delighted. Now let me see. There's always the washing up.'

'That wasn't quite what I had in mind.'

'You surprise me.' Ralph pealed with laughter. 'As a matter of fact that gives me an excellent idea. I have to go and see one of my parishoners tomorrow who has a bit of a problem. I'll ask her if she minds if I bring you along. I'm sure she won't.'

'Why does washing up remind you of her?'

'Because that is her problem. She has become an obsessional washer of hands. She makes them raw with it. Her sister is in despair. The local hospital wondered if I could help. I have had some previous experience of this problem and it requires quite an expenditure of time and dedication. That's where you possibly come in Jules.'

'And don't go out much from the sound of it.'

Ralph roared with amusement at Jules's sally. 'That's it in a nutshell. I'll be in touch tomorrow, have no doubt.'

Ralph whistled out as briskly as he had entered, starting an exaggerated limp halfway down the drive when he remembered his disparate shoes.

'Poor old man,' Peter shouted through the window.

Ralph pretended to prepare to vault the gate and then thought better of it. Instead he tripped over the little step and went sprawling.

10

Next morning Jules received the summons to be at the vicarage at eleven o'clock. He presented himself with mixed feelings, but at least he had some feelings, he mused to himself; not the empty void of no emotions; that was the worst of all.

Ralph was wearing a tweed suit of light greenish-grey colour. He appeared to be the suit's second choice of wearer, or even third. The suit clung to Ralph's bony, bent figure with the determination of a man hanging from the cliff edge by his fingernails. The trousers gave up the struggle halfway down his calves and the turn-ups were strained to bursting. The jacket exerted a bracing effect on the shoulders, which were wrenched back so that Ralph's arms hung despondently from their sockets, clearing his flanks by an unnatural margin.

A ray of joy swept over Jules when he beheld the sight.

'Ralph. You look magnificent. How long did it take you to choose that suit. You must have been inspired at the time.'

Ralph eyed Jules shrewdly and a broad grin developed.

'How kind of you to notice. There are so few of us with taste in these sartorial matters.'

'Sartor Resartus.'

'And the same to you.'

'It must have taken some considerable time to encumber yourself with it. I once saw Engelbert Humperdinck with such a tight-fitting suit on the stage at Bournemouth and he confided to us that it took him half-an-hour to get it on. Mind you there was a thunderstorm at the time which might have helped to shrink it for him. I remember we were wringing out our socks in the theatre. He didn't say how he would get it off.'

'I have to wear this suit,' Ralph confided, 'because it was given to me by the dear ladies we are now going to visit. You may know them. Molly Perkins is the twittery little spinster who lives in that cottage at the edge of the village. Her widowed sister Susan lives with her.

Molly has always been rather eccentric. Precise in her ways but latterly she keeps washing her hands so that they become raw. You will see. So that's it in a nutshell.'

'It isn't the only thing in a nutshell judging from your posture Ralph. We had better get on before gangrene sets in.'

'We set out before gangrene sets in. Very neat.'

'I thought it a suitable remark.' Jules grinned and leapt out of the way of Ralph's friendly cuff.

A front-room curtain ruffled as they went up to the sisters' front door.

Ralph and Jules stood under the little porch and waited for the door to open. Both sisters appeared. Molly was small and mouse-like, with a pointed face; her eyes had a wary look. Susan was stouter and more bland. Both were menopausal and flushed readily, as now.

'Come in Vicar. And Mr Osk. That is your name I believe? The vicar told us you were coming,' Susan said.

Molly smiled and nodded. They were ushered into the front parlour which was neatly set out with four easy chairs facing the window and a table set back on the rear wall with cups and saucers at the ready.

Molly disappeared and they heard the tap in the kitchen running.

Susan looked significantly at Ralph. 'You see what I mean Vicar.'

Ralph nodded. Molly reappeared and Jules noticed her hands were red and chapped. She sat down with them. Silence reigned. Ralph fidgeted in his seat.

'Is the suit comfortable Vicar?' Molly enquired. Her face was earnest and betrayed no irony.

Ralph cleared his throat. 'Perhaps a little tight here and there Molly. But very nice.'

Ralph undid the coat button and the two sides of the jacket sprang apart with evident relief both to themselves and to Ralph.

'That's better, isn't it Vicar?' Susan said.

Ralph wondered how to broach the subject of Molly's compulsion. 'Your hands look sore Molly.'

'They are Vicar. Gets worse as the day goes on.'

'That's because you will keep washing them Molly,' Susan said sternly.

'I have to. I don't feel easy unless I do. There's so much dirt around, and so many germs. My hands feel dirty. I must keep washing them.' She looked determined.

'Do you use handcreams Molly?' Jules asked.

'I can't. The creams get contaminated and I have to wash them off.'

'Well Molly,' Ralph said decisively, 'the doctor has told me that it can help if someone is here to try to stop you always washing your hands. Sometimes the anxiety gets less rather than more.'

'I've tried that Vicar,' Susan said. 'It doesn't work.'

'I know it's not easy. That is why Jules has come. To help you. Isn't that right Jules.'

Jules had been watching carefully and nodded.

'You have to speak rather distinctly ladies, because young Jules here is a bit deaf, but he can manage if you mouth your words. Isn't that so Jules?'

Tea was brought in and over the cups Ralph expounded what he knew about Molly's problem.

'This condition, an obsession, usually occurs in people who have always been rather meticulous.'

'That's her all right,' Susan commented.

'Then something upsets them, increases their tension and away they go. Some people spend ages setting out their clothes in a certain fashion, some keep clearing their throat in a certain way. These are called obsessional rituals. Then some have obsessional ruminations, certain thoughts keep recurring.'

'For goodness sake don't put any more ideas into her head,' Susan exclaimed.

'Oh Susan, don't be so silly,' Molly laughed nervously. 'I'm not that bad.'

'Well anyway it seems as though it's quite all right to try to prevent people going through all their rituals. It's called apotropic therapy, a turning away.'

'I'm to be an apotropic agent, is that it?' Jules enquired.

Molly looked doubtful. 'I have to wash my hands. I shan't feel clean otherwise.'

'Well feel dirty then.' Ralph spoke decisively. 'Feel dirty and see what happens. There are germs everywhere, as we know. Many of them are friendly and keep out the nasty ones. How about the parable of the devil who was cast out of the room and it was filled with seven much worse devils? I believe they are even treating some chronic infections by implanting non-pathogens to shoulder the pathogens out. How's that for biblical and scientific expertise in one succinct packet. I'm not just a pretty face you know.'

'Certainly not.' Jules laughed.

'Do you mean not just or not at all?'

'A knotty problem. Let's not try to unravel it.'

Susan had been sitting by, smiling, and even Molly was showing less tension. Her taut face had relaxed a little and her hands had unclenched.

Ralph stood up. 'I shall leave you now. I have other fish to fry.'

Jules rose and went over to him before he left the room. He held his arm lightly.

'I'll do what I can,' he said to Ralph, 'but it's all new to me I'm afraid.'

When Ralph had gone Jules stood for a moment undecided. Susan and Molly gazed blandly at him.

'How do you feel Molly?' Jules enquired after a few moments.

'I feel I want to wash my hands but I don't feel too bad.'

'Could you hang on as you are for say half-an-hour?'

'I think so. We'll give it a try anyway.' Molly managed a smile.

'That's great,' Susan said.

Now that Ralph had departed Jules did not find it easy to

chat to the two sisters. He fidgeted uneasily and Molly seemed gradually to pick up his contagion of unrest. Her expression hardened and her hands resumed their clenched attitude. She stirred in her seat and started to rise. Jules looked at his watch. Only ten minutes had elapsed. Twenty to go, he thought.

'Come on Molly. Let's have a stroll in your garden. You can show me what's there.'

Molly thrust past him. 'I must go to the toilet. You can't stop me doing that.'

The other two heard the loo door bang shut.

'Susan. Does your loo have a wash-basin in it?'

'No it doesn't.'

'What shall we do when she comes out? Shall we let her wash her hands then?'

'I suppose we had better,' Susan replied. 'That's normal enough after all.'

'Yes I agree. But should we start another half-an-hour after that?'

'I think we had better, otherwise she may pull this one every time.'

'Right,' said Jules.

Molly emerged and went to the kitchen to wash her hands. She reappeared in the living-room doorway looking pleased.

Jules came up to her. 'I am afraid we shall have to start the half-an-hour again Molly. It's only fair.'

'That's right,' Susan added.

Molly looked angry and shook her head.

'Oh come on Molly. Play the game. Let's go for that stroll.'

Jules propelled her outside but in five minutes they had exhausted the interests of the garden and were back inside. The minutes seemed laggard to all three of them and after twenty minutes Molly stood up once more. She made towards the door.

'Where are you going Molly?' Susan asked.

'Mind your own business.'

'But it is our business.' Jules rose and went towards Molly. 'Are you going to wash your hands?'

'I have touched my shoe and must wash my hands.'

'I'm not going to let you Molly for another ten minutes.

Surely you can wait for ten minutes?'

'I'm going now.' Molly headed for the kitchen.

Jules turned in despair towards Susan, who shrugged her shoulders, and then he made a dive for Molly. He caught her round the waist and held fast. Molly screamed and struggled but Jules would not let go.

Susan came up. 'Perhaps you had better let her Mr Osk. She seems desperate.'

'It's only for another few minutes Molly,' Jules implored. 'Please.' He hung on.

Molly continued to struggle. She writhed and twisted and Jules found himself hanging on more and more tightly.

'You're hurting me Mr Osk. Let go I say.'

'You must wait. All our efforts will be useless otherwise.'

Suddenly Molly lowered her head and bit Jules's hand. He cried out but maintained his grip.

'I'm going to see this through if it's the last thing I do.'

Molly looked down and saw the blood spreading from Jules's hand onto her dress. She gasped in horror.

Jules hauled her back into the living-room and struggled her into a chair. He released her and looked at his watch.

'Only seven minutes now.' He got out his handkerchief and bound it round the wound.

Susan seemed paralysed with horror and stared. Molly started to cry and they froze in a tableau of miserable endurance.

At last the half hour was up.

'You can go and wash now Molly,' Jules announced quietly. 'Well done.'

Molly's eyes fixed on his hand. 'I don't want to till I have looked after your wound. I'm truly sorry Mr Osk. I don't know what came over me.'

'That's just what we're trying to get rid of Molly, what comes over you, whatever it is.'

'Well it shows it can be resisted,' said Susan. 'You've lasted the half-hour.'

'Yes, but look what's happened,' Molly said.

'If it's done any good I don't mind at all.' Jules undid the handkerchief and inspected the wound. 'It's not bad anyway.

84

Just a deep graze.'

Molly went over to see. 'I'll give it a good clean and put a proper dressing on.'

'You can wash your hands for that,' Susan said.

'I should hope so,' Jules added.

☆ ☆ ☆

When Jules related the events to Ralph later in the day and concluded by telling him that it ended by their asking Molly to wash her hands, Ralph was filled with joy.

'It's to be a whole hour tomorrow,' Jules added.

'I should wear gloves then,' Ralph said with a wink.

11

Boris's concert in Sheffield had been greeted with ample but not rapturous applause. He himself was conscious of a technical mastery which lacked the lyrical element which had been eluding him recently, try as he did to infuse it into his playing.

He suspected the reason was not unconnected with his determination to put the affair with Jules behind him and press on with his own life. He was not the first to find that if the emotions get left behind by a willpower permanently in overdrive then either the willpower falters or it hardens itself to a diamond edge which cuts away all impediments before it.

Fiona met him in the foyer of the concert hall.

'Well done Boris. Not a note wrong. Not that I could detect anyway.' She smiled and fingered the air with a pianist's motions.

Boris hesitated. 'Maybe. And yet . . .'

'And yet what? Aren't you happy about it? I thought the audience loved it.'

Boris shrugged. 'I suppose so.' He sighed. 'What would you like to do now?'

Fiona looked mildly surprised. 'Well I should think some form of celebration is in order, isn't it? You haven't dragged me all the way up here just to pack it in at this stage and say cheerio, have you?'

A note of irritation was evident. Boris felt a steely resolve to show her what he was made of but the attendant pleasure was not there.

'Right.' He clapped his hands. 'I'll bet the hostel canteen will

87

be shut so shall we have a proper meal out somewhere?'

'I thought you were never going to ask.' She smiled and they set off.

The sky was clear and showed that purple haze which towns suffuse into the heavens above them when their illuminations are on. They linked arms and walked along the pavements. Many of the shop fronts were still lit up, their goods on parade like so many street tarts, available but at a price.

This notion occurred to Boris and he laughed out loud.

'What on earth are you laughing at?' Fiona gazed at him quizically.

'It's nothing.'

'Oh go on. It must be something.'

'Well, if you really want to know I was thinking you can't win, you either get VD or VAT.'

'I still don't follow.'

Boris sighed. 'It was a silly notion really. I was comparing shop goods on display with prostitutes. Both can be bought but perhaps the cost is more than one bargains for, VD or VAT. Do you see?'

'What a horrible thought. I'm sorry I asked you now.'

'Ask no questions, hear no lies, I saw a Chinaman . . .'

Fiona shook her head angrily and pressed ahead. Boris felt resentment slipping quietly in through the chinks in his *amour-propre*.

They passed several pubs and clubs blaring their presence with garish lights and harsh sounds and then saw a discreetly curtained restaurant with soft lights and quietude.

'How about that?' Fiona asked.

'Looks all right to me.'

The restaurant was half full. They were directed to a table near the entrance.

'We'll have a table further back please,' Boris heard himself say with a tone of inflexible determination which startled him.

They sat down. Fiona gazed at Boris with a look Boris felt to be challenging him, as if to say 'What have you got to say for yourself now, you big mouth.'

He frowned slightly.

'You don't look very pleased with yourself, or is it with me?' Fiona demanded.

'Why shouldn't I be pleased with you? Of course I am,' Boris retorted.

'You've no reason not to be, I'll say that.'

'Oh you'll say that, will you. "No reason not to be." Isn't that one of those double negatives which hide a positive.'

'I don't know. It's too clever for me.'

Just then the waitress appeared. 'Have you decided yet?'

Something in the way the waitress addressed them irritated Boris.

'You might well say yet. I'll give up yoghurt the day a woman can make a quick decision about a menu.'

'And what is that supposed to mean?' Fiona hit back.

She exchanged knowing looks with the waitress. The latter flounced and smiled.

Boris felt his irritation mounting. 'It might save time if you tell us what is off,' he said.

'Well, I'm going for the chicken,' Fiona said at once. The waitress nodded.

'And I'll have the Wiener Schnitzel,' Boris added hurriedly.

The waitress smiled. 'That's the one thing that's off.'

'Typical,' Fiona said before she could check herself.

'Typical. Why on earth typical? What do you mean? Is that what you think of me? A cross-grained oaf?'

'You're behaving like one at this moment.'

The waitress was staring at Boris with a tinge of disdain as the only expression visible on her face.

This fuelled his anger further. He pulled himself together with an effort.

'All right, I'll join you with the chicken.'

The meal passed without further incident and they paced back to the hostel with easy, leisurely strides. This time the shop fronts went unheeded. They felt no need to communicate and were content to let the streets lead them gently to their destination.

The corridor was empty and Fiona inserted her key in the lock. The mechanism was stubborn and Boris grasped her hand with his and gripped it tight.

'Ooh, you're hurting Boris. I can do it.' She shook him off.

He put his arm round her waist and pulled her to him.

She resisted. 'No Boris. I'm going to bed.'

She turned to the door and gave the key a firm wrench. It turned and the door opened.

'What's the matter. Don't you like me or something?' Boris sounded angry.

'It's not that. I just want to get to bed.'

'Well I think I deserve more than that.' Boris pushed her into her room and followed her in. He stood there uncertain what to do next.

'Get out.' Fiona flung the door wide open and stood by it.

'Oh well. If that's the way you want it. There are plenty of other fish in the sea.' He shrugged his shoulders and departed.

Fiona breathed a sigh of relief.

12

Jules found over the next few days that Molly could last for lengthening periods of time between one hand washing and the next and after a week of daily attendance he decided that he could leave Molly and Susan for a few days.

'You're doing well, Molly,' he announced breezily. 'I think I shall abandon you, for a few days at least.'

'You mean to say you can manage without our cups of tea?' Susan laughed. 'Surely you must be addicted to them by now. Let me see, how many have you had?'

They all laughed together.

'Just as well you don't feel you have to wash your hands after each cup of tea,' Jules observed, 'but seriously, do you feel more able to stop yourself washing your hands so frequently?'

'Yes, I'm much easier now. I don't feel that terrible urge to wash them. Unless they're obviously grubby, that is.' Molly waved her hands aloft.

'I'll take that as a wave goodbye, for the time being at any rate.'

☆ ☆ ☆

Next morning Jules was up early and gazing idly out from his bedroom window, feeling more carefree than for some time.

He listened to the familiar morning medley of sounds and was about to turn inwards from the window when he espied Fletcher hurrying down his drive. He was strangely garbed in a mackintosh from all the openings of which protruded, severally, pyjama collar, sleeve cuffs and trouser ends. A man for all seasons, Jules mused.

Even more bewitchingly Fletcher was carrying his recording apparatus which had obviously been hastily assembled and from which coils of flex dangled and swung dangerously. A large loop trailed along the ground and Jules gasped as he saw Fletcher's foot tread on it, giving a sudden jerk to a piece of the equipment he was holding. Fletcher appeared to go through the contortions of a spastic juggler before he could right himself.

Just then Jules observed Rev. Ralph Dene emerge from his church and saw him burst out laughing when he spotted Fletcher. He could just manage to hear their voices in the morning silence.

'Hello Fletch. If you're hoping to record me I'm afraid you missed it.'

'No, no Ralph. Quick, help me. I'm sure I heard the cuckoo, over there.' He pointed beyond the church.

'But it's September man. You can't have heard it. It was probably my cuckoo clock.'

'You haven't got one, have you?'

'No. Of course not. I was only joking.'

'Well quickly, help me then. I have just been reading that some birds nest again in the autumn and it was suggested that the reason was that the length of daylight in the autumn is similar to that in the spring and some birds get fooled into going through their spring routine again.'

'So you think your cuckoo has been taken in by it. I should have thought his voice had broken. They make a very funny cracked call in June. I should think by now they would sound like Louis Armstrong after a night on the tiles.'

'It would be extraordinary. That's precisely why I want to record it. Quick, give me a hand.'

Jules felt intrigued and could not hear enough to satisfy his curiosity. He hurriedly dressed and joined the other two. They had not progressed far. They each stood, statuesque and poised, ears straining for any further sound of deluded cuckoos.

'Hello. Are you posing for something or is it a new form of yoga, for more elderly gentlemen perhaps?' This evoked two furious hisses of disapproval.

'Shusshh. We are listening.'

'Did you say you were listing?' Jules knew they hadn't really said that. He pretended to straighten them. Then he made an exaggerated pantomime of looking round.

'What are you up to now?' Ralph enquired.

'Where's the sculptor? You must be posing for your statues. That's it, of course. Harlequin and Columbine.'

'Have you heard a cuckoo?' Fletcher hissed urgently. 'About half-an-hour ago now.'

'I have heard, well two cuckoos, as a matter of fact.'

'Where man, where? Quick now. In which direction do you think?'

Jules smiled. 'It was more recent than that. Just now, in fact. Right here.'

Ralph screwed up one eye and grimaced with the other.

'Young fellow, I've got some work for you. When we've finished the business in hand, that is,' he added hurriedly, glancing anxiously at Fletcher.

They waited a while in silence.

'Well if the wretched creature isn't going to oblige then I suppose that's it,' Fletcher said morosely.

Ralph patted him on the back. 'Never mind Fletch. The path of true scientific enquiry never did run smooth. Let's help you back with your stuff.'

When they had returned Fletcher and his equipment safely to base Ralph turned briskly to Jules. 'Jules, come back for a cup of rectorial tea and I can ask you about Molly.'

They went to the kitchen. Ralph poked his head into the hall and shouted up the stairs, 'I've brought young Jules back for a cup of tea and to enquire about Molly Perkins.'

Jules related the progress he had made. While he was doing this Ralph picked up a pair of large and venomous-looking cutters, inspected them closely, brandished them in the air and executed a series of snapping lunges at all and sundry.

Jules looked on in astonishment. He concluded his narration abruptly.

'What on earth have you got there Ralph? You haven't taken up circumcision as a side-line have you, by any chance?'

Ralph pealed with laughter. 'I don't think the mothers would let me within a mile of their precious bundles with this in my hands. Mind you I could employ you with a bottle of sal-volatile. You could catch them as they fell and revive them with your little bottle while I did the necessary. How about that?'

Ralph grinned and made a few more passes with the cutters, this time accompanied by fencing movements of an indeterminate nature.

Just then Winifred appeared. 'What on earth are you doing Ralph cavorting about like that?'

The untended kettle was enveloped in steam. Winifred glanced disapprovingly at it.

'Why hasn't it switched itself off I wonder?' She moved over to it and switched it off.

'You do have to wet the tea with it you know. You have to put them together, boiling water and tea leaves before you get tea. Do you savvy?'

Ralph winked at Jules. 'What should we do without them?'

'As I am not plural, only one of me as you might say, though I sometimes think you imagine there are more, I fancy you must be referring to the tea leaves when you say "without them" '.

'Just a figure of speech dear. A fine figure, if I may say so.'

'But what are those cutters for?' Jules put in. Ralph sat down and took a cup of tea from his wife. He motioned Jules to sit.

'I may not be up to circumcision, but I can sink lower. I do cut something off. Guess what?'

Jules pondered and then sniggered.

'Much lower,' Ralph added sternly, eyeing Winifred.

A look of relief appeared on Jules's face. 'Toenails,' he said triumphantly.

'They may be toenails to you but they are onychial appendages to me and my friends. My friends cannot always see their onyxes. In some the stomach hogs the foreground, in others their legs won't bend so the nails are always far distant and others cannot hold this instrument firmly enough. The chiropodists are worked off their feet.'

'Off their feet but onto others,' Jules interjected.

Ralph continued, 'and I volunteered, after a few instructional

94

sessions, to help them out. Today is my day for trimming. Would you like to accompany me to see what goes on? Then if I couldn't manage it for any reason, and you happened to be free, you might be able to help out.'

Jules hesitated.

'Christian duty and all that,' Ralph added, gently but firmly.

'Don't let him bully you,' Winifred warned.

'Well, come and see anyway. Can you come back at ten and we'll set off? I promise I won't get you too involved but it's better to be a bit too involved and trim back than to mope with not enough to do.' He smiled at Jules and made a pass at Winifred with the trimmers. 'Anyone for a hair cut?'

Jules rejoined Ralph as arranged. He could not entirely hide a look of mirth, which Ralph spotted.

'Why are you grinning, or rather trying not to grin?' Ralph enquired with an exaggeratedly innocent expression.

'You must admit you do not look as if you caught the 8.30 to town every morning. No pinstripes and all that.'

In fact Ralph was wearing his dog collar and clerical jacket but beneath that his knobbly knees protruded below a pair of khaki shorts. He wore long socks with a boy scout label on them and brown non-lace slippers. Partly hidden inside the dog collar the folds of a handkerchief could be seen circumscribing his neck.

'There is a logical explanation for everything if you think my garb a little eccentric. I will explain in order to defuse any further inclination to levity on your part young Jules. The dog collar and jacket are to proclaim my authenticity. As pieces of flying nail are apt to get down behind my collar I have inserted a handkerchief as a buffer. I am always having to kneel down for which purposes long trousers are an encumbrance and I am frequently having to remove my shoes to shake out bits of nail, hence the ensemble.'

'You've certainly nailed it for me. Thanks for the exposition.'

'Not too exposé I hope. I am decently covered, I trust.' He swung the plastic carrier bag. 'My equipment is in here.' The cutters could be seen jutting dangerously through the bag.

'Is that bag adequate Ralph? It looks to me as though you are going to lose your cutting edge if you're not careful.'

'You must keep a watch out for me Jules. A sharp lookout.'

The first house they approached was a little thatched cottage set back down a winding path. Ralph disappeared round to the rear and beckoned Jules to follow. He tried the back door. It yielded a little but was still stuck. Ralph drew back and lunged at the door with his shoulder.

The door resisted and Ralph drew back, puffing. 'Always have trouble with this one.'

'Let me have a go.' Jules stepped forward.

He turned the knob, put his shoulder to the door and at the same time shoved the lower part of the door with his foot. The door opened innocently.

Jules bowed gracefully to Ralph. 'After you.'

'Clever Dick.' Ralph tapped his head.

'No. It's the foot you use on this occasion, not the head.'

A female voice could be heard from within. 'What are you up to Mr Dene? I know it's you. You're the only one who has trouble with that door.'

Ralph grimaced at Jules.

Mrs Brewstock was a plump sixty-year-old. She was reclining on a couch and two massively swollen legs were ranged on a seat. The top of her feet were also grossly swollen and thickened discoloured toenails were growing from the toes.

'I'm in position, as you see. Ready and waiting.'

'Just as well I've brought a chaperon then. This is Jules Osk. He is helping me out today. And as a matter of fact he was helping me in, now I come to think of it.'

'I thought you got in quicker than usual Mr Dene. No offence meant, you know.'

Mrs Brewstock's shoulders heaved with mirth and her flesh trembled. She wiped her eyes.

'If I could give you a bit of my flesh it would help me and you too, from the look of it. Those knees of yours don't look ready-made for too much kneeling. In your profession I should think well-padded knees were a requisite.' She shook with

96

laughter again.

Ralph drew out his cutter. 'Now then to the nitty-gritty.'

'You be careful with those Mr Dene.'

Ralph knelt down and attacked the nails with his cutters. The jaws clashed together with harsh snaps and pieces of nail flew across the room. Suddenly the parrot in its nearby cage let out a loud squawk and flighted its wings agitatedly.

'You've felled it Mr Dene. My poor Polly. There, there. Did the nasty man hurt you then?'

Ralph broke off. 'Phew. I'm sorry about that Mrs Brewstock. Never got a bullseye with him before have we? Must be on form today. Have you got a handkerchief Jules? Mine's otherwise employed, as you know.'

'Yes I have,' said Jules cautiously. 'Why do you ask?'

'I was wondering if you would do a sort of matador act with it, hold it up like a cape in front of Polly's cage like a good fellow.'

Jules duly obliged and Ralph finished off his snipping.

'That's it for today then Mrs Brewstock. See you in a month's time. Sorry Polly.' Ralph wiped the blades clean with surgical spirit and blew a kiss to the budgerigar before he and Jules withdrew.

'Now we've got a bit of an ordeal.'

'How so?' Jules asked.

'The next customer is what you might call the archetypal awkward customer. Mr Clews is a real old curmudgeon. Bony, miserable and cross-grained. He enjoys it I think. I always adopt an aggressively jocular attitude with him. I think it floors him a bit and it saves me from getting angry. We'll see what happens.'

Mr Clews lived in the end house of a terrace of red brick and slate-tiled houses. His end, clumbered with corrugated iron sheds and a detritus of old, rusted bicycles and gardening tools, contrasted emphatically with the other end, which was festooned and wreathed with hollyhocks, giant daisies and lupin stalks at this time of year.

Ralph breezed in. 'Hello Mr Clews. Who lives at the other end of your terrace?'

'Why do you want to know?' Mr Clews squinted suspiciously at Ralph.

'I just wondered. Is there a woman in the house at that end?'

'What if there is? What's it to you then? Eh?'

'I thought it had a woman's touch, that's all.'

'And this end doesn't, eh? I can't get about like some. Takes me all my time to keep body and soul together.'

'Glad to hear you manage that.'

Ralph paused and fought off the temptation to add 'You could have fooled me.'

Mr Clews frowned and muttered at the fire which smouldered disconsolately in the grate.

'We've come to cut your toenails Mr Clews, Jules Osk and I. Let's be seeing them.'

'You can take them with you for all I care.' Mr Clews growled.

Slowly, with groans and grunts, Mr Clews exposed his nails. They were thickened and brown and tortuously curved.

Mr Clews eyed them balefully. 'The beggers give me gyp.' He spat at them contemptuously.

Then he aimed another gob of spit at the fire, which hissed back angrily. 'That's what I'll be I expect. Roasted in hell like that gob.'

'Now, now. That won't do. How about seeing you at church? I'd get someone to fetch you and bring you back.'

Mr Clews showed signs of alarm. 'I start coughing when I go outside. It's bad for my chest.' He gave a protracted hawk.

Ralph got down to his task and clipped away. Suddenly he cried out, dropped the clippers and clasped his hand to his right eye.

'What's the matter?' Jules asked anxiously.

'A piece of nail must have hit me in the eye. It stings like billyho.'

Ralph held his eye for some time. Mr Clews stared impassively at him.

'Let me have a look.'

Jules helped Ralph up and lead him to the window. He eased

98

Ralph's hand away. Ralph blinked and tears rolled down from the eye. He blinked a few more times.

'Oh, that hurts.'

Jules prised the lid open gently. 'It looks bloodshot and I think there's a cut in the eye. We had better get you to the hospital casualty.'

'I suppose so,' said Ralph reluctantly. 'What a nuisance.'

'I'm always a nuisance.' Mr Clews added morosely. 'Everything about me's a nuisance. You might as well do away with me.' He stared into the fire.

'I had nearly finished.' Ralph called back as he and Jules left.

Ralph held a handkerchief to his bad eye with one hand and Jules led him by his other hand.

In casualty Ralph's aspect, already somewhat bizarre before the accident, was now sufficient to attract attention and led to a more rapid passage through the toils of the casualty department than usual.

He was ensconced in a cubicle and a young doctor soon appeared.

'What seems to be the trouble, er Mr Dene? A clergyman I see. Got a beam in one's eye, or is it a moat, I forget.'

Ralph smiled feebly. 'It feels like a moat. A big one at that.'

'What happened?'

'I think a piece of toenail has flown into my eye. It's jolly painful.'

'Let's have a look.'

After his examination, the doctor called for some forceps, inserted local anaesthetic and presently brandished a small chunk of nail before Ralph's good eye.

'I'm sure that will feel better now that that little blighter is out, but you've got a small cut on the conjunctiva so I'll put some drops in and a pad over and ask you to get someone to repeat the drops as instructed.'

When Ralph arrived home Winifred sighed. 'I might have known it. You were in far too flippant a mood today. Something like this was bound to happen.'

13

The next day was one of those heavy, negative days. The sky stretched endlessly, like an implacable grey mantle, no wind stirred and the columns of bonfire smoke rose like disconsolate pillars, with no zephyrs to play with them.

Jules hurried round to the vicarage. Ralph was sitting in his study listening to the wireless. The daily paper lay crumpled and abandoned at his feet. He greeted Jules warmly.

'Just the man. I'm delighted to see you, even if it is through well certainly not rose-tinted spectacles. You don't realise what you'll miss until you miss it.'

'That's a convoluted sentence. I suppose it has a meaning when it's unfurled.

'Furl yourself into a chair anyway.'

'How is the eye?' Jules asked, peering at the pad. 'Is it sore?'

'You'd better ask it. How are you eye? Are you sore? "Ay, Ay" he said. No, as a matter of fact this pad is very comfortable. Winifred has been putting the drops in and all is well.'

'Would you like me to take you down to the hospital when you have to go?'

'That would be most acceptable. Thanks Jules. And how are you? I think I'll take this opportunity, if you're agreeable, of having a chat with you about things.'

'Oh. What things?'

Jules pretended to look surprised but he knew really. Ralph was not one to fail to offer counsel when he conceived it was needed and Jules had to admit that it was needed.

'You have got a very big problem to handle Jules. I know

101

that. But there is someone to share your burden and that's our Lord. Will you let me help to put you in touch with him? I wish you would. He is such a strength to me.' Ralph put out his hand and held Jules's arm gently.

Jules hesitated. 'That's just the trouble Ralph, in a way. It worries me that we tend to turn to God, if there is one, when we need something. How can you be sure that he is not just a, what shall I say, a wish-fulfilment? It's nice to have him around, like a father figure, ready to help us when we cry for help.'

'I know there is that,' said Ralph. 'Obviously it comes down to belief in the end. There's a difference between thinking something and believing something. If you believe something then there's an emotional charge goes with it. I believe in God and life after death and there it is.'

'And I'm afraid I don't. Not in life after death, anyway. And if you don't believe in life after death then all the rest of it becomes pretty futile. I'm sorry.' Jules paused.

They sat quietly for a while.

Then Ralph continued. 'Jules. Would you be prepared to come to some evening classes I am holding this winter about the fundamental Christian beliefs? I wish you would.'

Jules pondered for a while. He spoke slowly. 'I do need help. I would love to believe but I just don't.'

'For some belief comes easily,' Ralph said. 'For others it is slow and hard. And of course some never do. But if you don't study it and think about it then religion doesn't stand a chance.'

'I certainly think that mankind needs something like the Christian religion. We seem to be making a right muck of things without it. Yes Ralph, I will attend, unless I have a concert of course. I shall have to sit up front to hear but I am learning to lip-read almost unconsciously.'

☆ ☆ ☆

Next Sunday at St Swain's Church Jules seemed to find more significance in the service and felt a gentle contentment he had not felt before. He wondered about it.

102

After the service he spotted Fiona putting on her coat and went over.

She looked up and smiled. 'Hello Jules. How are you? That was funny over those owls wasn't it? I've had many a laugh since.'

'Me too. I wonder what on earth Fletcher and your Dad will get up to next?'

'Goodness knows.'

'Shall we go for a cuppa?'

'I'd love to.'

Just then Boris passed by. He looked petulant and his face lean.

Jules pondered at the gentle feeling he had inside himself and wondered what effect such a feeling would have on Boris's face if it were in Boris. Not much, he supposed. He wondered whether to ask Boris to join them and decided to leave it to Fiona.

Fiona was wondering the same thing and decided to leave it to Jules, so neither spoke. Boris hesitated and wandered off.

'Come on,' Jules said softly, taking Fiona's arm. 'I'm rather glad we're on our own.'

'So am I.'

'Great,' said Jules and felt it.

Over supper he related to Fiona his plans with Ralph and had her pealing with laughter over the nail cutting.

'He's such a card,' Fiona said. 'I love people who get stuck into things.'

'What, even blind alleys?'

'Blind alleys or deaf alleys. It doesn't matter.' She looked intently at Jules. 'You didn't mind my saying that I hope?'

Jules paused and looked directly at Fiona, who was watching him anxiously. He spoke slowly and deliberately.

'No, I didn't mind. I've got to face up to it but it's not easy.'

Fiona extended her hand across the table to him.

'I realise now, or am beginning to realise at least, that I've got to replace what I lose by my deafness with something else. My hearing will go. I have to accept that because I don't believe in miracles so I've got to replace it. I even had a small example of that with Ralph. There he was, unable to do his usual tasks because of his padded eye, so he turns to and chats with me. That's constructive as far as I'm concerned. That's what I've got to do. Get stuck into something I can do, whether I'm deaf or not.'

'That's it. And I'll help you. If you want me to?' She looked anxiously at him.

'There's nothing I would like more in the whole wide world,' Jules said and Fiona thought she detected a tear in his eye.

She looked away with a little sigh of contentment and the steam from their cups of coffee plumed gently and blended in the air.

14

Fletcher Pemberton was brooding. His organ restoration work was in temporary abeyance and at such times, Doris knew, his mind would range far and wide until it lighted on some target. He would then become abstracted and disappear for prolonged spells to the library. Sometimes small clues as to the likely direction of his thoughts would appear and sometimes a large clue would manifest itself like a thunderbolt.

Doris was washing up in her kitchen after lunch one day when she heard the unmistakeable squeals of a pig. She peered from the window and beheld Fletcher marshalling a large reddish-brown pig down the ramp from a lorry. The pig rapidly disappeared round the side of the house hotly pursued by Fletcher.

The lorry driver closed up the ramp and waved to Fletcher. 'I'll be off,' he shouted down the drive. 'I reckon you'll have your hands full right now.'

A shudder passed through Doris. So that was the reason for Fletcher's activities at the bottom of the garden. Doris had learned not to enquire too closely otherwise she was apt to become involved with Fletcher's schemes. But a pig. Had he dropped any clues? She pondered. There had been a cutting taken from the paper a while ago. Now where was that? Doris rummaged on Fletcher's desk amid the paraphernalia of papers and suddenly spotted the picture of a pig. The headline read 'Pigs on the scent of drugs.' Under the picture it read, 'Lower Saxony's first sniffer pig, Luise, goes to work on luggage at Frankfurt.'

A large dark pig was portrayed thrusting its snout into a carrier bag, surveyed by a complacent customs official. So that's why he has been so concerned with drugs hauls, she mused. Whatever next?

Presently a breathless Fletcher appeared. 'Hello,' he said.

'Hello. Having fun and games are we?'

'What do you mean?'

'You seem breathless. Was that really a pig I saw you shepherding into the back?'

'Shepherding is hardly the word Doris. Yes it was a pig, a Tamworth.'

'And what on earth do you want with a Tamworth, or a Gloucester Old Spot, or a Landrace or whatever? Not to eat I hope. We'd never get through it and anyway I know you couldn't bear to eat it once you were looking after it.'

'You're quite right Doris. No. I'm going to train it to sniff out drugs. They're used in Germany already you know.'

'I know. I saw the cutting.'

'I wonder if Gilbert would help me? I could do with a bit of a hand.'

'Well don't look this way my lad.'

☆ ☆ ☆

Gilbert Blake readily agreed to help and appeared the next day. His sturdy figure was swathed in an old-fashioned smock, with pleated ruffles and loose sleeves. His moustache rode proudly above with its darker hue.

'Good heavens,' Fletcher exclaimed. 'For a moment I thought it was Stalin. Gave me a nasty shock.'

'Flattery will get you nowhere. Well, you told me the task involved handling a pig so I came accoutred accordingly.'

'I must say you look quite cute, "accutered" you might even say. Where's the floppy hat then?'

'Can't be found. This used to be my grandfather's. He was a shepherd at one time.'

'It might have been helpful if you had brought a crook. No such luck I suppose?'

106

'No. You'll have to do with just me and my hands. What's afoot?'

'More a question of trotters,' Fletcher said.

He outlined his plans to train Sniffer, which was what he had christened the pig, to detect smells and eventually the smell of drugs.

'I believe they like truffles,' Gilbert said.

'So I am told, but hardly a helpful remark here. We have to train Sniffer to unearth certain objects by their smell and then reward him with a nice meal.'

Fletcher and Gilbert set about arranging boxes, crates and old suitcases in a pyramid at the bottom of the garden, positioning it over a bowl of warm mash which Doris had prepared. Then Fletcher strode up to Sniffer's shed and swung the door open. They waited expectantly.

Grunts were heard from within and Sniffer made a tentative appearance at the doorway. He raised his snout and wrinkled it, dilating the nostrils as he did so. Finally, with a grunty squeal, he set off determinedly in the direction of the pile of boxes, wagging his little tail and swinging his buttocks.

'He's got the scent,' Fletcher whispered in awe.

Sniffer nosed his way round the pile and then gave a shove at one of the weaker sections of the edifice with his snout. The boxes trembled for a moment at the outrage and then, slowly and gracefully, tumbled over onto the startled pig, who turned tail and tore off past the side of the house, through the gate which Doris had inadvertently left open and into the road.

Ralph was passing on his bike on his pastoral rounds and was astonished to find a pig hotly pursuing him.

Fletcher and Gilbert ran into the road and Fletcher shouted to the vicar, 'Stop him Ralph. There's a good chap.'

Ralph applied his brakes and came to a standstill astride the bike, undecided as to the best course of action. It was not a situation he had been called upon to cope with before. Sniffer was close at hand and looked to Ralph entirely determined to proceed on his way whatever Ralph might do to prevent him.

Ralph made a split-second decision, leapt off his bike and projected a flying rugby tackle at Sniffer's neck. He clung on grimly and was dragged along for some yards before Sniffer came to a reluctant halt. Ralph gasped and beamed proudly at Fletcher and Gilbert who had arrived on the scene.

'You should tackle round the ankles Ralph. Didn't they teach you that at school? That's a foul tackle. Could be dangerous.'

'To the animal or me?' Ralph enquired. 'I rather felt this was the preferable end under the circumstances, the end justifies the means, don't you know.'

'I can see what you mean. Well done anyway.'

As they were strolling back, Sniffer safely held by one ear by Fletcher, Ralph started to chuckle.

'What's so funny Ralph?' Gilbert enquired. 'Nervous stress or something. Has your bravery been at too great a cost?'

'I was just thinking,' Ralph said, 'that they talk of a vicar and his flock. Some flock, two humans and a pig. Not a bleat among you.'

Sniffer gave a loud snort.

'I think he heard,' Fletcher said. 'Very sensitive creatures.'

'And,' Ralph continued, 'you chaps don't read your papers, otherwise you would be aware that we are breaking the law.' He paused enigmatically.

'How so?' Gilbert asked. 'We seem perfectly sedate to me. Walking quietly along the public highway in a restrained manner. No nuisance to anyone.'

'Ah, but pigs must be kept on leads when on the public highway.'

Fletcher said in astonishment, 'You must be joking, surely. On a lead? Pigs on leads? The world's gone mad.'

'No. I'm deadly serious. Owing to the risk of spreading pig disease, blue ears and all that, the Ministry of Agriculture has decreed that owners must apply for a certificate to allow them to take the pigs for a walk, and then only on certain designated routes, and the pigs must be on leads.'

'And I suppose there's a fine if they foul the pathway. Is that it?' Fletcher sounded incredulous. 'Shall we all be walking on Sundays with our pigs on leads, fluttering our certificates and gathering up the effluvia with our little spades?'

'You may mock,' Ralph went on, 'but people are keeping

Vietnamese Pot-bellied pigs as pets. They're very cuddly, I'm told, and can be used as hotwater bottles on cold nights.'

'Good heavens. Now I've heard it all,' Gilbert exclaimed.

'I doubt it,' Ralph muttered ominously.

Sniffer was reproved, released into his quarters and fed generously with mash and leftovers.

Ralph stood · fascinated. 'Devotion. An important part of human activity Fletcher. I do not imagine pigs are troubled by the tribulations which assail my flock. My devotion to them is not so easily administered. For one thing their appetite for my offerings is more unpredictable, even non-existent at times, and for another there is disagreement on the menu I should feed them with.'

'I wouldn't have your job for all the tea in China,' Fletcher smiled. 'But come in Ralph, and take a cup of tea with Gilbert and me.'

Over the tea their minds ranged freely and easily, as is the way with mature and independent men who have surmounted their chief obstacles and have come to survey the remainder of the field with a degree of complacency.

'I've a problem with obtaining small amounts of drugs for my tests, or rather Sniffer's tests,' Fletcher observed.

Ralph nodded and then a huge smile replaced his air of earnestness. The others noticed and wondered what would come next. They were prepared to wait and let it unfold. Ralph continued to smile and then moved his head slowly from side to side. Still there was silence. Then he chuckled. Shortly afterwards Fletcher and Gilbert started to chuckle. This appeared to startle Ralph and he looked first at Fletcher and then at Gilbert.

'A trifle rude, isn't it, for one's host and his friend to start chuckling at the expense of a guest?' Ralph feigned pique and glanced sternly at each of the others.

'Do you want to know what Gilbert and I were chuckling about Ralph?' Fletcher said. 'Do you really want to know?'

'You tell me.'

'We saw you chuckling first and you kept it to yourself. We knew you would be dying for us to ask you what was amusing you, we both realised that without telling each other, and took you on at your own game, and began to chuckle ourselves. Now we have told you why we were chuckling you can jolly well tell us why you were. The suspense is killing us, isn't it Gilbert?'

'Almost,' Gilbert laughed.

'Hoist with my own petard eh?' said Ralph. 'Do you really want to know why I was chuckling?' He burst out laughing until he choked. 'I was imagining your experiments ending up with one drug-dependent pig and two jailbirds.'

'Is that what you would call a happy outcome, since you were laughing?' Gilbert enquired.

'I would come and visit you in jail. I could try out my next sermon on you. There's a promise.'

'That might be an excellent ruse to empty our jails,' Fletcher said. 'Promise that all prisoners would be visited by their spirited and spiritual vicars and subjected to their next sermons. What an idea.'

'My sermons are not that bad, surely Fletcher?'

Fletcher screwed up his face and closed his eyes.

'Ecstasy, I see. It takes many forms,' Ralph said. 'As a matter of fact I do know a bit about drugs and the law. I had to look into this some time ago. Pin your ears back and I'll expatiate.'

Fletcher darted up and fetched an ashtray for Ralph.

'I don't smoke, Fletch.'

'I thought you said you'd expectorate.'

'No, I'll expostulate though if you don't sit down and listen.'

Fletcher and Gilbert assumed exaggerated poses of attention and Gilbert put his knuckles up to his forehead and bent his head forward.

'All right Rodin,' Ralph went on. 'I shall take some time so I hope you get cramp. You deserve to. There are five schedules of so-called Controlled Drugs: one, those with no medical role, such as cannabis and LSD; two, opiates; three, barbiturates; four, benzodiazepines; five, compounds containing small quantities of two. Have you got that? These can only be obtained on prescription. However the Home Office may issue a licence to possess synthetic substances which have a similar odour but do not possess the other pharmaceutical effects.'

'Phew, the man's a walking encyclopaedia,' Gilbert exclaimed.

'Well I'm going to see my GP and ask him for a bit,' Fletcher said.

'I don't think he'll let you have any,' Ralph said.

'I'm going to try anyway. No time like the present. I'll go and ask for an appointment, this evening if possible.'

Fletcher went to the phone and was given a cancellation.

'Five-fifty,' he announced on his return. 'Are you coming Gilbert?'

'OK'

'I'm off.' Ralph rose and shouted goodbye to Doris.

She came out into the hall. 'Goodbye Ralph. Did I hear Fletcher arranging to see our doctor?'

'Er, yes,' Ralph left hurriedly.

Doris strode into the living-room. 'What's this I hear about you seeing Doctor Stewart?'

'Oh, it's nothing dear, nothing at all.'

'You weren't injured by that pig were you?'

'No, no. Certainly not.'

'It's something to do with that wretched animal though, isn't it?'

'Yees, in a way.'

'Why are you being so secretive? What are you hiding?'

'You'd better out with it Fletcher. There's nothing to hide really anyway,' Gilbert said, looking extremely innocent.

'If a woman's instincts could be harnessed to sniff out drugs we could put old Doris out in the shed,' Fletcher laughed, 'and have done with it.'

'And you would be content with warm mash and leftovers in the kitchen would you? I don't think.'

'We have a problem,' Fletcher said seriously, 'about how to obtain or acquire the small quantities of drugs we need for our experiments. You haven't any hidden away in secret recesses, have you Doris? Little stocks of pick-me-ups for a rainy day?'

'Certainly not. I'm beginning to see the light. You are going to try to bludgeon poor old Dr Stewart into giving you some.'

'Bludgeon wasn't quite the word we had in mind, was it

111

Gilbert? Interest in, persuade, even cajole at a pinch, but certainly not bludgeon. Far too crude an instrument.'

'Well, I don't think you stand a chance. Not an earthly.' Doris suddenly darted for the door and made for the phone.

Light dawned on Fletcher and he scrambled out after her. 'No you don't. I'm not having you forewarn him. Leave it to our mature and sensible judgement.'

'That's the trouble.'

☆ ☆ ☆

At the appointed hour Fletcher and Gilbert were to be seen in Dr Stewart's waiting room. Fletcher's number came up. 'Are you coming in with me Gilbert?'

'Surely not.'

'Oh do. You will lend weight to the occasion. An emblem of our commitment.'

'I've been called many things in my time but never an emblem of commitment before. I think it suits me, don't you?'

'When you two have finished procrastinating outside my office would you do me the courtesy of entering and thereby saving my time.' Dr Stewart's voice could be heard through his door, which was ajar.

'Sorry Doctor. May I bring a friend in?'

'You can bring the Prince of Wales in for all I care as long as you come in, for God's sake.'

'Not an auspicious beginning.' Gilbert whispered and made to retreat.

'No you don't,' Fletcher grasped him firmly by the arm and propelled him in.

Dr Stewart remained seated at his desk. He was in his sixties and had grey close-clipped hair, a small grey moustache below grey penetrating eyes, and the sharp look of a heron standing at the water's edge.

'I don't often see you Fletcher, I'm glad to say. Are you nervous that you bring an escort. What's wrong with Doris?'

'She hasn't rung you Doc., has she?'

'No. Not that I'm aware. It's as serious as that is it? You look remarkably fit for someone whose wife may have to ring and who needs to bring a friend with him. I take it you are a friend?'

'Oh I'm sorry Dr Stewart. Yes, this is my friend, Gilbert Blake.'

'He's privy to all your little secrets, is he?'

'He's privy to this one.'

'Which one?'

'That's what I've come about.'

'I thought we were never going to get there. How many more are waiting outside, would you say?'

'That's a crafty one Doc. Is that how you hurry us along? We have come about my pig.'

Dr Stewart looked far from pleased.

Fletcher hurried on. 'It's all in the public interests. I am trying to train a pig to sniff out drugs. They're doing it in Germany, but I need small quantities of opium, LSD, cannabis and that sort of thing. Can you suggest any way how I can get a bit?'

'You mean to say you've come here wasting my time on such a fool's errand? What do you think I am? A purveyor of drugs for all and sundry? I've got sick people waiting outside while you badger me with your trivial and flippant request. Get out.'

'Oh Lord. I'm sorry Dr Stewart. Doris was right. She warned us not to come.' Gilbert nodded assent.

'Oh she did, did she?' Dr Stewart paused. 'Well, she was right. It's neither in my power, nor is it my wish, to grant you such a request but perhaps I have been a bit sharpish on you. Shake hands and call it quits, shall we?'

On their way out Dr Stewart called to Fletcher and Gilbert. 'Try ringing the Home Office. They might be able to help.'

113

15

Jules started to attend Ralph's evening classes on the place of Christianity in modern society.

Ralph would stride in and pace before them, his eyes luminous, seeming to encompass them all in their sphere. Sometimes both bicycle clips would remain at their posts round his ankles, cuffing his trousers, sometimes one would be there and one not. Sometimes his jacket would be open and sometimes buttoned, with the button occupying the hole belonging to its neighbour as often as not.

Jules found himself fascinated to speculate the precise form of anomaly Ralph's dress would manifest that particular day. His thoughts wandered along those lines, for he found it hard to hear all Ralph uttered.

'How are you getting on?' Ralph asked him one evening.

On this occasion Ralph's cardigan had squirmed its way through a gap between the jacket buttons and had become enmeshed in a button hole. Jules had watched fascinated all evening to see whether the errant fold would escape but it did not. He resisted a strong urge to release it.

'Well actually Ralph, I'm finding it a bit difficult to hear. You talk rather quickly and I can't always see your lips. You will keep dodging about.'

'The artful dodger am I. Maybe I had better chat with you in my study. How are you getting on Jules?'

'I'm still getting requests for concerts but it is becoming increasingly difficult for me. Boris, you know, my pal Boris Striman, is doing very well.'

'Yes, I heard about him. I'm glad you are still friends Jules. Very glad indeed. And Fiona? Do you still see her?'

'Oh yes. We all get on fine.'

'Get on fine sounds a bit lukewarm Jules. Would you like it if we all got together, all five of us?'

'You mean all four of us don't you Ralph?'

Ralph laughed. 'That was deliberate. Partly to make sure you were hearing me and partly serious. There is the presence of God to consider. Do come along. Ask the others too. If you give me a choice of one or two evenings I am sure we can fit it in.'

'Thanks Ralph. I'll be in touch and I'll opt out of these evening classes here then.'

☆ ☆ ☆

Boris was not keen on giving up an evening but Fiona persuaded him and some days later all four met in Ralph's study. It was dusk as they chatted and settled.

By this time Ralph had perched himself on the side of a chair. Jules was opposite, seated more sedately where he could see and hear to the best advantage, and Fiona and Boris were comfortably slotted onto a settee. Ralph was too experienced a hand to let the awkward pause which is apt to develop at such a stage in the proceedings have any chance of establishing itself.

'If we had a piano in the house I would have loved to hear you two boys play but, alas, we shall have to deprive ourselves of that, shan't we Fiona?'

Fiona felt his brown, alert eyes sweep over her. She felt in their expression a power she had not noticed before. She gave a slight shudder.

'Are you chilly?' Boris enquired.

'No, no, I'm not. I can't think what it was. I'm not chilly, I promise you.'

She pulled her cardigan across her blouse and straightened her skirt.

Ralph was now standing by the window. Fiona watched the outlines of the garden fade from a dusky yellow to grey, which darkened and enveloped the outlines of the trees and borders as

Ralph talked volubly, excitedly.

'I have asked you all to come here this evening to discuss certain matters about life and at the same time to help Jules, our friend here, over a few hurdles. I have a strong, no, fervent trust in Our Lord and I happen to believe his teachings and examples can provide the answers we all seek in our lives. My aspiration is to inculcate these beliefs into you. Quite how one does this, or how I do it, is often a problem, but I have noticed that at times of stress the human spirit cries out for succour, and at such times is ready to listen. Hence our gathering this evening.'

Ralph became more agitated as he expounded his doctrine and the other three began to glance uneasily at each other. Ralph noticed the little tiltings of the head and shoulders, the expressions of slightly detached indifference, even of disdain, with which people communicate.

He paused and frowned. 'I think it would be better if I separated you three to pray on your own and I will come to each of you in turn.'

He motioned Jules and Boris to leave the room, ignoring any signs of dissent, and stationed Jules in his small study and Boris in the dining-room. He bade them pray on their knees with such stern intensity that they obeyed without question.

He returned to Fiona in the sitting-room and moved across to draw the curtains.

Fiona found herself shuddering again when she heard the harsh scraping of the curtain runners and saw the abrupt, almost fierce tug with which Ralph completed the motion. He turned to her and his eyes seemed to bore into her. She felt they blurred out her clothes and her body and were focusing on her soul, like a tomogram.

'We must pray,' he said.

He came towards her and Fiona flung herself onto her knees. Ralph rested a hand on her shoulder and she suppressed another shudder. He knelt beside her and prayed aloud.

Presently he paused. She heard a catch in his breath and then little sobs. She felt his arm grasp her waist tightly, pulling her over onto him and then he released his hold and lay prostrate

117

on the floor, moaning softly.

'Ralph, Ralph. What is it? What's wrong?' She tried to pull him up.

'Such thoughts were going through my mind Fiona. Such terrible thoughts.'

'I know Ralph. I felt them. I understand.'

'I don't think you do. You can't. I don't know what came over me.' He struggled to his feet. 'Will you ever forgive me?'

The door opened and Jules looked in. 'What is going on?'

Ralph straightened his crumpled clothes. 'Excuse me,' he said and hurried out.

Jules glanced enquiringly at Fiona. 'What on earth's happened?'

'It seems we all have feet of clay.' Fiona sat down heavily and tried to smile.

'You don't mean poor old Ralph got a bit carried away, do you? Not him, surely.'

Fiona nodded. 'Well, nothing happened really. But I felt it. It was there, the old male lust. There's nothing else to call it, I suppose. It's terrible.'

Boris appeared. 'I can't go on praying for ever. I see you two have finished. Where's Ralph?'

'He'll be back soon,' Jules said.

They waited uneasily. After some minutes they heard Ralph's steps outside. There was a short pause and he entered. He had composed himself and smiled. His regard lingered on Fiona.

'I think we have had enough for one evening,' he said. As he shook hands they all noticed his damp palm and the slight tremor in his grip.

'Poor old chap. He seems overwrought,' Boris said. 'Powerful stuff religious conviction.'

Fiona and Jules said nothing.

118

16

Fletcher contacted the Home Office and, after the grinding into gear of the official machinery, was put in touch with Sigma Laboratories who provided him with small quantities of substances having the smell but not the narcotic effects of the regular drugs.

'Iso-osmic and non-narcotic,' he told Tom MacDonald, the publican of the Ploughman, Fletcher's local.

'Blimey,' Tom exclaimed from behind the bar. 'That's a good one. Nearly as good as the Leith police dismisseth us.'

'I never could say that,' said Fletcher, 'drunk or sober.'

Tom lowered his face into his pint and froth clung to his Kitchener moustache. He blew it off dismissively and leant his massive arms across the counter.

'I've seen a bit of smuggling in my time in the navy, but not on the scale of nowadays. It's a disgrace.'

Two youths further down the bar looked across at his words.

'Talk about hypocrites,' one said loudly to the other. 'Here he is selling drugs in glasses and yet he criticises other drugs. Bastard.' He turned his back on Tom and Fletcher.

Tom moved down the bar.

'I'll have no more of your cheek, young lad.' Tom thrust his face over the counter.

The youth shrugged, and Tom returned to Fletcher.

'I think I'm ready to put Sniffer, that's my pig, to the test now. I've been training him in my back garden and I think he's got the idea all right but we need to test him out under different conditions.'

'I've just the idea.' Tom's face brightened. 'Do you know Jack Pullman?'

'Can't say I do.'

'You must have seen him in here. Red face, grey hair and rather pointed nose. Usually sits over there.' Tom gestured to a corner. 'Often has a black Labrador dog with him.'

'Oh I know. I've got the man.'

'Well, he's a retired customs official and his dog's a trained drug detection dog. The dogs are given by the public to the RAF and then they train them, either for drugs or explosives. It's usually one man per dog and when the bloke retires he often takes his dog with him. See?'

'I do see.' Fletcher looked interested. 'Do you think I might have a word with him? Perhaps we could organise a little contest between Sniffer and his dog. What say you?'

'Sounds a great idea. I'll ask him when he next comes in and, if he's game, I'll tell him to get in touch with you.'

☆ ☆ ☆

A few days later Fletcher answered his doorbell and found Jack Pullman and Rip, his dog, at the door.

'Good evening. I'm Jack Pullman.' He shook Fletcher's hand. 'And this is Rip.'

'Hello Rip,' said Fletcher. 'Funny name for a dog.'

'I know. Can't think why. Something to do with when we were training him I suppose.'

'More like preventing others tripping if you can stop them taking drugs. Won't you come in.'

Doris was introduced and they sat in the sitting-room with cups of tea, Rip lying sprawled, with his legs stretched forward, by the side of Jack's chair.

'Has it been easy training Sniffer?' Jack enquired.

Doris hid a smile behind her hand. Fletcher looked across at her and grinned.

'There have been moments of, well, shall we say frustration,' he said.

'Let's say exasperation, or even desperation,' Doris added.

'I know. Only too well.' Jack said. 'It takes about nine weeks to train a dog but you have to keep re-training them after that.'

'How do you get them interested?' Fletcher asked.

'We use a training aid, a hollow tube which they love to retrieve, a sort of game. That's the reward. Then we introduce the substance into the training aid so, in the end, they associate the smell of the drug with finding it.'

'Do you have one particular drug for one dog?' Doris asked.

'No. Heroin, cocaine, amphetamines and cannabis, all four categories. Cannabis is easy, a good strong smell, but heroin has what they call a slow plume. The smell takes longer to percolate through the wrappings, but it does, in the end. The dogs have to be nearer for that.'

'I wonder if Sniffer might be better with the hard ones. The difficult ones to smell, I mean, not the hard drugs.'

'I couldn't say.'

'Could we try it Jack? Would you be willing to pit your Rip against my Sniffer?' Fletcher looked excited.

Jack allowed a grin to spread slowly across his face. 'What a notion. I'm game. How about you Rip?'

Rip snorted and wagged his tail briefly.

'Is that assent?' Fletcher asked.

'As much as you'll get likely.'

'Great. Where shall we have it?'

'Could I suggest somewhere other than our garden.' Doris gestured towards the garden. 'The Waste Land is all very well in its place on the printed page, but not so funny in my back garden.'

'There has been a certain, shall I say, "going over", since Sniffer arrived,' Fletcher admitted.

'I know you have to turn the sod,' Doris said, 'but there's a limit.'

'Shall we see if Tom will let us use his back garden?' Jack suggested. 'He's just starting to set out the tables and chairs for the summer. Should make a good venue.'

121

Tom did not receive the news with quite the same enthusiasm as Fletcher and Jack, but the prospect of the extra custom such a contest would promote won the day and a Saturday evening jamboree was arranged.

On the Saturday in question Fletcher and Jack went to Tom's beer garden in the afternoon to set the scene. They decided that the bottom of the garden, beyond the tables and benches, would be the best site for the contest between Sniffer and Rip. They rolled eight barrels and casks of different sizes down near the hedge and set them up in two rows of four. In the barrel second from right at the rear they placed a small quantity of the target substance, well wrapped.

'Do you ever get any drug-addicted dogs?' Fletcher asked.

Jack laughed. 'Not that I recall. The drugs are usually too well hidden and packaged for them to be got at by the dogs, but now and them a dog does break into a packet. We then wash out his or her stomach pronto with saline and send for the vet.'

'What happens if your dog has a cold?' Fletcher asked. 'Can it still sniff out the drugs?'

'They get a bit snuffly at times but they still seem to manage. We don't work them for a couple of hours after a meal, though.'

'Why's that Jack?'

'They're not keen enough. No go.'

They made a final adjustment to the barrels.

'Surely the smell of stale beer will put them off?'

'No. One scent carries another. They'll still find it.'

That evening "The Ploughman" was teeming with the local worthies. Tom and his staff skeltered amongst the tables and benches carrying trays laden with amber, frothy pints which caught the last rays of the sun.

Jack made a quiet entrance with Rip but was soon spotted and greeted boisterously.

'Good old Jack. Atta boy.'

'Where's the porker then?'

'Last minute training, I shouldn't wonder.'

'What's the odd's then Tom?'

'No betting allowed.' But Tom knew when he was crying into the wind.

At length Fletcher was sighted leading Sniffer proudly down the road. He had fixed a Union Jack halter round the pig's neck but, for good measure, he kept a tight grip on Sniffer's left ear, the halter being somewhat loose.

'You should have a ring in his nose,' someone shouted.

'He doesn't want to risk spoiling his chances.'

Fletcher ignored the jibes and strode over to Jack.

Rip evinced signs of curiosity and went over to circle Sniffer cautiously, flaring his nostrils at the pig from time to time. Sniffer stood and flicked his tail.

'We don't put dogs straight to the suspected target,' Jack told Fletcher confidentially. 'We let 'em work up to it, have a few sniffs elsewhere first, and if they find other scents, let them have it for a bit. They'll soon come back. But when they get to the real stuff then they stick like limpets.'

'Sniffer's not so fast as Rip,' Fletcher said. 'Rip will have a head start or more.'

'All right. I'll start Rip from the back and you can take Sniffer much nearer.'

'Fine.'

A suitable forward spot was designated for Sniffer and both animals were pointed in the ·direction of the barrels. Tom was poised with his 'Time Gentlemen Please' bell, and at the signal he rang it.

Rip was motioned forward by Jack and bounded ahead. He passed a hesitant Sniffer and Fletcher gave his pig a shove from behind to set him on his way. Both animals reached the front row of barrels and crates and Rip excitedly scampered round them.

Sniffer hesitated and then thrust two barrels aside and made unerringly for the second, rear barrel on the right. Rip joined him and began to bark and wag his tail. He scratched furiously at the sides of the barrel, rose up on his hind legs and pushed the barrel over. Sniffer seized his chance and charged the end of the barrel.

There was a splintering sound and Sniffer disappeared inside the barrel followed closely by Rip. An agitated scuffle could be heard and Sniffer's squeals mingled with Rip's barks on the evening air.

'We must get them out.' Jack ran up with a bucket of water and sloshed it into the barrel.

The cacophony increased.

'Let's tip the barrel up,' Tom suggested.

Out tumbled Rip and Sniffer, the package between Rip's teeth. Jack prised it away. Sniffer stood undecided as to his next move.

A cheer went up from the audience.

'Who won then?' A furious argument broke loose which continued far into the night. Fletcher, Jack and their charges slipped away unnoticed in the turmoil.

'Who did win, do you think, Jack?'

'Dunno. Shall we call it a dead heat?'

'If we do and go back to that pub we'll be dead meat.'

'Let's go and have a quiet pint at The Boar's Head.'

17

'Your eyes are darting everywhere'. Mary leant forward at the breakfast table.

Peter lowered his paper with a rustle. 'Golly. For a moment I thought you could see through my paper.'

'I can see through you and you're thicker.'

'Thank you very much.'

'Now, now you two,' Jules smiled at them.

'I mean you Jules,' Mary persisted. 'There was a time when your level of attention was, shall we say, rather low at breakfast.'

'But now I'm the life and soul of the party, is that it?'

'Not quite, Jules. But I've noticed how you watch things attentively these days.'

'There's a reason for that Mother. I have found there are a myriad little signals we all give off which we normally don't notice but which I find help me very much in lip-reading and picking up what people say. For instance I can usually tell when someone is about to speak by a little tensing of the hands or a deep breath. What they are saying will show by their facial expressions, whether it's sad or fribaldibous.'

'What on earth's that?' Peter put down his paper.

'It's a mixture of frivolous and ribald. Rather good, don't you think?'

'Good for what?' Peter chided.

'What are your plans today?' Mary asked.

'I shall practise as usual and then I'm going off to the Wigmore Hall. Franco Paster wants to fix up a concert, possibly

125

with Boris and myself, to sort-of make up for the fiasco last time.'

'That horrible place,' Mary shuddered, 'I never want to go there again.'

'Do you think it's wise, Jules?' Peter gazed earnestly across the table. 'You might find it upsetting.'

'I've thought about it Dad. I may not get the chance for any more concerts there and, after the publicity of the last one, we could get a good turnout. After all that's the be-all and end-all of the exercise, isn't it?'

'Not really. I know you've got to live and, as a concert pianist, therefore perform, but surely there's much more to it than that. Appreciation of music, pleasure for your friends, and for you. That sort of thing.'

'Oh, I know Dad really. I don't mean it strictly but nevertheless my chances of performing in the Wigmore Hall after this time are not likely to be all that great, so I must seize them when they offer.'

'It's a bit like the hype on a book I suppose. The more the notoriety the better the sales.' Mary put her hand to her mouth. 'Oh, I didn't mean that really, it sounds nasty. I just meant . . .'

'I know Mother. A little notoriety, as you put it, gains more attention than any amount of expertise. I have to agree with you. Funny old world, isn't it. But we have to take it as it comes. That's why I'm going to do this concert if I'm asked.'

'Good lad.' Peter patted Jules on the arm.

☆ ☆ ☆

The concert was arranged for a few months hence. Boris and Jules sat in Franco Paster's office. Jules recalled the previous time when he had confronted the two girls from the Booking Office and they had not been able to identify Boris.

'How shall we arrange it?' Franco asked. 'I suggest one of you does the first half and the other the second. But who shall do which?' He rubbed his hands and looked enquiringly at them.

Boris and Jules raised their eyebrows at each other and

spread their hands in gestures of indecision. Each was trying to gauge in his mind which would be preferable, to go first or second.

'You'd better decide Franco,' Boris said.

'Very well.' Franco paused. 'I can't decide. Let's toss a coin. Agreed?'

'I suppose so,' Jules said. 'Seems the fairest way.'

Franco spun a coin.

'Heads Boris first, tails Jules first.' He peered down. 'Heads. You're first Boris. You can each have forty minutes. Let me know what you select as soon as you can, please.'

☆　☆　☆

Jules and Boris agreed on a concert of straightforward classical pieces.

'Stop short at the Romantic era, eh?' Boris had said. 'Suits me fine.'

When Jules came to reflect on this later he decided this arrangement would suit Boris, with his technically perfect style, more than it would suit him.

As the urge of competition worked within him, fuelled by consciousness of his growing deafness, an imp entered his soul. I'm going to show them, he thought. I'll play some really flamboyant pieces: Charles Ives or Mussorgsky, something like that.

☆　☆　☆

The day of the concert arrived. Fiona had come along and both Jules's and Boris's parents were present. They were all sitting in the front of the hall.

Boris played his classical pieces with correctitude and met with restrained applause.

When Jules started to play his flamboyant pieces Boris's expression of satisfaction gradually changed to one of anger. He leant across to Fiona in the pause between the pieces and whispered to her. Mr and Mrs Striman picked up his disquiet and became unsettled themselves. Peter and Mary listened complacently as Jules poured his soul into the music, concluding with some of Chopin's Etudes.

There was a moment of hush when he finished followed by the spontaneous applause of an audience genuinely moved.

When he turned and acknowledged them he noticed a short row of motionless people: Boris, Fiona and the Strimans.

As Jules went towards his parents he felt a fierce tug on his arm.

'You cheated,' Boris hissed at him.

'I decided to change what I played, that's all.' Jules knew he was in the wrong.

'We'd agreed to keep it classical and you didn't. You cheated. I shall never forgive you.' Boris glowered at Jules for a moment and stalked off.

Jules's feeling of triumph vanished and a cloud of remorse descended. Has it come to this, he thought, that I have to cheat over my friends in order to hold my own?

'Well done old chap.' Peter beamed.

Mary touched his arm and smiled. Then she sensed something was not right.

'What is it Jules? Are you all right?' She mouthed her words over the hubbub.

'I'm all right Mother. I suppose I'm all right.'

'It's the reaction, I expect. Time we got home.' Peter guided them out.

When they arrived home they sat in the kitchen. Mary made the tea and plonked the pot down carelessly. She knew something was wrong.

'What it is Jules? There's something.'

'I cheated Mum.'

'What do you mean you cheated boy? You did fine. They loved it. Much better than the first half. Boris was all right but you really showed them what you can do.'

'That's just the trouble Dad. That's why I cheated. We had agreed on straightforward classical pieces but I changed that without telling anyone, even Boris. Don't you see?'

'Oh, I see. And he feels you stole a march on him, is that it?'

'That is it and I did steal a march on him. I cheated and the whole world will know.'

'Oh surely not Jules.' Mary tried to soothe him.

'Yes they will. You just see.'

Jack Stringer, perhaps wishing to compensate for his unfavourable review of Jules's last concert at the Wigmore Hall, was lavish in his praise of Jules and dismissed Boris's contribution in a few sentences. This served as salt in Jules's wounded self-esteem and he descended into despair.

Ralph came round to see him in response to the Osks' request.

'Come on old chap. Buck up.'

Jules was slumped in a chair, his eyelids drooping, his arms dangling over the chair arms.

'Isn't it enough if I have to put up with my deafness? Now I've added deceit to it. Piling Pelion on Ossa.'

'I'll pile prayer on, on,' Ralph hesitated, 'oh, on prayer, if you don't pull yourself up, or at least let God and me pull you up.'

'I can't. My whole life is useless. If I can't hear what's the use?'

'Plenty of use. Look at Beethoven. Everyone knows he was deaf but listen to his music. Some people think the suffering he had enhanced his music.' Ralph looked earnestly at Jules.

'It won't do. I know you're trying to help. You don't understand. In fact Beethoven's piano playing, and he had been a wonderful player, got worse and worse. He banged too hard on the loud notes and was too soft on the soft notes. In the end his conducting failed too. He was trying to rehearse the first act of *Fidelio* and got slower and slower. The orchestra followed his timing and the singers stuck to the proper time. Schindler had to scribble him a note to tell him to stop. Poor old Beethoven was so upset that he rushed home, covered his face with his hands and wouldn't speak to Schindler until suppertime. Does that sound as though he coped all right? No, I'm finished.'

'No you're not. You've made the very point yourself Jules. In spite of all that Beethoven went on composing, didn't he? And what compositions. He did what he could do and didn't do what he couldn't do. Simple, eh?' Ralph wagged his head at Jules.

'What can I do then?' Jules showed no sign of starting to respond to Ralph's encouragement. 'Nothing in music I imagine, and that's what I've trained for.'

'I don't know so much. Look at Elizabeth Glennie. A deaf drummer. What do you make of that? She's learnt to sense the vibrations and that helps her. I was reading about her the other day. You could help deaf people learn what they can about music and rhythm. I'll make a few enquiries and let you know. In the meantime don't give up Jules. Fight the good fight, do.' Ralph grasped Jules by the arm and pulled him from the chair.

Jules attempted a smile. 'I suppose you're right. I'll do my best. Thanks Ralph.'

As Jules had feared a letter from Boris appeared in *The Times* a day later. It read: 'I note your Musical Correspondent's report of the concert Jules Osk and I gave at the Wigmore Hall on Wednesday last. Praise was lavished on Jules Osk for his spirited interpretation of fresh and demanding pieces whereas my performance of classical pieces, well-known to most of the audience, was passed over with little comment. It might be thought that there is little more to say about such familiar works. I wish it to be known that in performing such recent and demanding compositions as Jules Osk chose he was breaking an agreement we had made that we would restrict ourselves to the classical repertoire. Yours faithfully, Boris Striman.'

'Oh dear,' Peter said as he read the letter at the breakfast table. 'This is what Jules feared.'

Mary read the letter. 'I only hope Ralph can come up with something.'

18

Ralph rose from his desk as Peter was ushered in by Winifred, knocking to the floor the manuscript which had been jutting over the edge as he did so. The paper floated gracefully down and came to rest across his shoe. Ralph bent to pick it up and hit his head on the desk edge as he straightened.

'Sorry,' he said.

'Was that remark addressed to Peter or to the desk?' Winifred said with a resigned smile.

'To you all. All and sundry.'

'I don't know where Mr Sundry is but here's Peter to see you.' Winifred left them to it.

'Sorry to disturb you Ralph but you may be able to guess why I have come.'

'Is it Jules? Poor old chap.'

'I'm afraid so.'

Peter started to clear some books which were occupying an armchair and Ralph dived across to help.

'I'm sorry.'

They both stood there laughing as they held the books and looked around vainly for a suitable resting place for them.

'There's always the floor,' Peter opined.

'Not too popular with Winifred, but a good suggestion nevertheless.'

Ralph's glance searched for an alternative site in vain.

He grinned. 'Under the circumstances an excellent suggestion Peter.'

The books were deposited in a corner and the men sat down.

'What Jules needs is something to take him out of himself. If his worries can't be ignored than they must be, what shall I say, softened by some other interest. I take it there is no possibility of cure or even improvement in his hearing, is there?'

Peter shook his head sadly. 'I'm sorry to say there is not. Not at the moment, anyway. Not at this point in time, to use a phrase I detest.'

'So do I,' Ralph said with conviction.

Ralph curled up in his chair deep in thought, his right hand clasped across his mouth so that his forefinger could twiddle with the curly strands of hair at his temples. His head was bowed forward and Boris could see the light from the desk lamp glancing off the bald crown.

Suddenly he straightened up and raised his right forefinger aloft. 'I've got it. Perfect. What brings out the best in people?'

Peter shook his head slowly. 'You tell me.'

'Why, helping other people. It never fails. And if they have similar problems then, in tackling one person's, I won't say in solving it, the other one benefits too. Don't you agree?'

'I think you're right Ralph.'

'Well I happen to know that there's a poor little lad who is going deaf and is having a hard time of it, both at school and, unfortunately, at home. His name's Philip Wilkins and he's only nine. If I can get those two together it's bound to help one or the other, and preferably both. I shall see to it, that is if you and Mary agree.'

'I certainly agree and I am sure Mary will too, but I'll ask her, just to be on the safe side. Then we can put it to Jules.'

'That's where the resistance may lie, I suppose. Who would be best to tackle him?'

'I think you Ralph with your, er, enthusiasm. You would be best.'

'Call it conviction and I'm your man.'

Ralph stood up abruptly and strode over to Peter. He hauled him from his chair and shook him vigorously by the hand.

'Let me know the time and place and I'll do what I can.'

132

Jules had listened to Peter and Mary without enthusiasm but the prospect of witnessing Ralph in action caused a little ripple of curiosity in him sufficient for the purpose and he found himself in Ralph's study the following afternoon.

Ralph paced up and down with his hands clasped in front of him. Jules sat listlessly in a chair.

'Life can be very difficult Jules. Oh, I'm sorry,' as Ralph noticed Jules straining to hear him. He came to sit opposite Jules.

'That'll cramp your style.' Jules gave a wry smile.

'How do you mean.'

'Immobility isn't your strong point, now is it Ralph?'

'Not exactly.' Ralph laughed and gave a lunge at Jules's shoulder.

Then he looked serious. 'I have known two people do exactly the same things during one day and at the end of it . . . what.'

'Twilight?' said Jules hopefully.

'Twilight and evening star. I'll give you evening stars, clever Dick. No. One of them reported a wonderful day and the other an awful day. Moral please Jules.'

'A little black cloud came and rained on one of them and the sun shone on the other.'

'That's not a moral conclusion, that's a weather forecast. But,' Ralph went on, 'it will serve my purpose very well. If you take the little black cloud to be a cloud of depression and the sun to be optimism then the point is made. How we feel about each day is very dependent on how we feel inside.'

'I suppose so.'

'And how we feel inside can be adjusted, altered; call it what you will.'

'Not so easy.'

'Perhaps not, but it can be done. One obvious way is through Christ. I should be remiss if I did not place that first, but I know not everyone, perhaps including you, can accept him, at least for the present.'

'So what then?'

'We all have in us,' said Ralph, unable to remain seated any longer, 'a coil of snakes hidden in a bag. Our emotions are like that, all intertwining and twisted up together, and every so often one rears its head above the others.'

'What a horrible notion. I don't like snakes much anyway.'

'Ah. That's just the point. You may not like them, or some of them, but you won't do yourself a service by ignoring them.'

'Perhaps not. Get bitten more likely.'

'Just so.' Ralph was triumphant. 'You must learn to be a snake charmer.'

'That's a bit tricky, isn't it?'

'Very tricky but well worth learning. I shall give you lesson one here and now.'

Jules pretended to look round the room.

'What are you looking for?' Ralph demanded.

'Your pipe. Surely all snake charmers, reputable ones anyway, have pipes.'

'Who said I was reputable? Redoubtable maybe. Now Jules, seriously, if you want to gain someone's attention what do you do?'

'Speak clearly as far as I'm concerned.'

'You pay more attention to their nearest likeness. Induce jealousy, then you gain their ear. So, what do you do?'

'Sharpen the knife?'

'No Jules. Please be serious, because I am. Now at any rate.' Ralph gazed earnestly at Jules. 'If you are deaf you find someone who is also deaf and you try to help them. Do you see?'

'And it so happens you have just such a person in mind, is that it Ralph.'

'You've taken the words out of my mouth.'

'Oh come on then, let's have it.'

'Have you heard of Philip Wilkins? He is only nine and is going deaf. He's finding it hard going. Do you think you could help?'

Jules paused. 'Does it really help if a non-swimmer dives in to help someone who is drowning?'

'We don't know what we can do until we try.'

'It's better to try and fail than not to try. Is that what you're saying?'

134

'Certainly, sometimes.'

'And now is one of those "sometimes" is it?'

'I rather think it is.'

Ralph contacted the Wilkins family and a visit by Jules was arranged.

Accordingly the next evening, after school, Jules knocked at the Wilkins' door.

Mrs Wilkins answered. She was plump and flaxen, with her fair hair tied up in a loose bun which gave the impression that it had somehow rolled down a steep hill during a temporary separation from the rest of her hair. Strands of hair protruded from its contours, many of them attempting to be miniature satellites of their parent, and in a few places more organic and fundamental upheavals of the contours of the bun were apparent, revealing exciting glimpses into the dark interior.

'You must be Jules Osk. Oh, sorry. YOU MUST BE JULES OSK.' Mrs Wilkins bellowed the repetition. Jules winced.

'Yes, I am Jules. If you will just speak towards me and let me see your lips move, then you will not need to shout Mrs Wilkins.'

'Sorry. Right you are. Come on in. Philip is expecting you.'

Jules was shown into the sitting-room.

A general disarray prevailed which included the furniture, scattered crockery looking like so many fossils of bygone meals and the company. Philip noticed three children, all intent on watching the television.

'Philip,' Mrs Wilkins shouted.

The two older children, a boy and girl, glanced up with annoyed expressions.

The youngest child must be Philip, Jules thought. He was seated next to the TV, his fair, sallow face watching the screen intently. The older boy threw a soft cushion at him and Philip looked up, startled. He glanced round and saw his mother and Jules. A fleeting expression of annoyance was rapidly replaced by a more sullen expression, his mouth set tightly.

'Come here Philip and meet Mr Jules Osk. He's come to help you. You remember the vicar spoke about him.' Mrs Wilkins enunciated the words with exaggerated emphasis.

'Oh Mum. Be more quiet please,' the girl said.

Mrs Wilkins gave her a withering look.

'Perhaps we had better have a chat somewhere else,' Jules said hesitantly.

'We've got a small front room, but it will be cold.'

'How about the kitchen then?' Jules asked. 'Or should we be in your way?'

'Oh I don't mind. Come on in there then.'

So far Philip had not spoken. Jules sat with him at the kitchen table while Mrs Wilkins busied herself here and there. Their conversation was punctuated and rendered more difficult by clangings, bangings and scrapings.

After one particularly loud bang Philip smiled ruefully. 'I can't hear much.'

Philip shrugged and looked at Jules's mouth. 'Nor can I.'

Another fusillade of clashes sounded as Mrs Wilkins took a saucepan from the cupboard and knocked over another one.

'I can hear some things though,' Jules added.

In the end it was decided that Philip should present himself to the Osk household at eight o'clock in the morning on Tuesdays and Thursdays for Jules to try to help him.

'We can't get him into town for the classes the clinic runs and anyway he misses too much school then. Though if he can't hear much of the lessons, that's no good either. I dunno. We can't afford to pay you Mr Osk. You can see how it is.'

'I don't expect payment Mrs Wilkins. I'm doing this for the vicar and of course for Philip, and for me.'

'For you? How come?'

'We'll see.'

Jules found he was spurred by the challenge of helping Philip, and Peter and Mary noted with approval the flurry of letters and telephone calls which he executed.

By the time of Philip's first visit he had found out many things about deafness which he did not know before or which he had been too indifferent to bother about.

Philip was wearing his school clothes when he presented himself on his first morning. He rang the bell and stood on the threshold with his school books in a satchel. Signs of a hasty breakfast were on his blazer and face.

'Hello Philip. Well done, come on in.'

Jules led him to the little room at the back where he studied and practised his piano, which stood in one corner.

Besides that there were a table, two chairs and a bookshelf stuffed with books.

'You'd better meet my parents.'

Mary and Peter greeted Philip warmly and then left.

'Can you hear if I speak clearly and you watch my mouth?'

Philip hesitated. 'I think so.'

Jules sat opposite Philip and clasped his hands on the table in front of him. 'You have got me going, you have Philip. Do you know that?'

'Going where? And I've only just got here.' Philip added with a flash of humour.

They both laughed. 'You're taking the mickey out of me, aren't you Philip? Admit it now. Call me Jules by the way. No need to stand on ceremony here.'

'But we're sitting,' Philip grinned.

'A little bit of a wag are we, eh? Well you'll get as good as you give master Philip, so I warn you. But we haven't much time. You mustn't miss school.'

'That doesn't matter. Fat lot of good it does me anyway.' Philip slipped back into his taciturn mood.

'Now, now. Listen to me. I have found out many things, some of them even helpful. There's a registered charity called Music and the Deaf based at Huddersfield. I'm very interested in that and the Mary Hare School for the Deaf in Newbury have an orchestra. Then there's The Beethoven Fund for Deaf Children; they provide special musical instruments which help with the rhythm and melody of speech. And of course all the many associations for the deaf such as The Royal National Institute for the Deaf in London and so on.' Jules paused for breath. 'Have you got all that?'

Philip grinned and pointed into his right ear with his right index finger and then away from his left ear with his left thumb.

'In at one ear and out of the other eh? But you do like music, don't you? Rev. Dene said you did.'

'I did. But how can I? It's daft, isn't it? As my pals have told me, you might as well ask a one-legged man to join an athletic club.'

'Might be useful in the three-legged race. There's always something one can do, whatever the handicap. I'm serious you know Philip.'

Philip stared at Jules. At first his face was expressionless but gradually animation crept in until he exclaimed, 'I do like music. I love it. If you can help me with that Jules, I'll, I'll, oo, I don't know what.'

'You can worry about "what" when I have helped you, so that's one worry you can put behind you at the moment. The next time you come I shall start to get down to details. I shall try to get you lip-reading and begin the music side of things. What instruments have you tried in the past?'

'I tried the violin a bit, but couldn't get on with it. I had a bit of a go on the drums too. That was better but it all folded up when my deafness got worse.'

'Right,' said Jules as he rose. 'I shall start you on the piano, for two very good reasons, because there's one here and because it's my best instrument, and we'll get you back on percussion too.'

Philip went off to school and the teachers noticed an alertness which the boy had not shown for a long time.

☆ ☆ ☆

Philip arrived ten minutes early for his next visit to Jules. He was soon settled in his chair watching Jules's face.

'What is music Philip?'

There was a short pause. 'Well, sound I suppose.'

'But what are sounds?' Jules went on.

Philip looked puzzled.

'They are vibrations Philip. Vibrations in the air. They're the essence of sounds and therefore music. Do you see the importance of that? The importance to you and me?'

Philip looked puzzled.

'The importance is,' Jules said with emphasis, 'that there are

138

other ways of hearing vibrations, well sort of hearing them, sensing them really, and these are ways we deaf people can develop more than someone with normal hearing can. A bit like a blind person developing very acute hearing.'

'I see,' said Philip.

'Now, I am going to show you ways of sensing vibrations. You probably know that the higher the frequency the higher the note, so there you are, a perfect way of taking in music, don't you see?'

'It's a bit difficult. Vibrations are not like hearing something. Can't be.'

'Well I can only tell you that many deaf people go to musical concerts with a musical score and get great pleasure from the vibrations which they receive from the playing while they read the score. Apparently it helps to wear light clothes and sit on wooden benches which resonate to the vibes. People have even tried holding balloons.'

Philip burst out laughing.

'You may laugh young feller, but I'm serious, I'll show you.'

Jules sang a loud middle C. Philip listened.

'Now place the palm of your hand on my chest.' Philip did so hesitantly. Jules sang the note again. Philip's eyes brightened.

'Do you get more "oomph" when your hand is on my chest?'

Philip hurriedly withdrew his hand and they both laughed.

'In today's climate I shall have to be careful Philip. Dear me, how the world has changed. We are all so suspicious of each other nowadays. Where will it end? Seriously though, was there a difference?'

'Yes,' said Philip. 'I can see what you mean; feel what you mean, rather.'

'Before you go I'm going to play the piano and I want you to concentrate on the vibrations. Hold your hands on the piano if you want. Better than my chest any day. Then go outside and hold your palms on the wall. See what you can feel.'

When Mary passed by she saw Philip with his hands pressed to the wall, concentrating hard. She went in to Peter.

'Have you seen what Jules has got Philip doing?'

'No. What?'

'He's standing in the passage with his hands up, pressed against the wall.'

'Good heavens. Is Jules inflicting some sort of strange punishment on the poor boy? Sound like something out of the Maze Prison to me.'

Peter tiptoed to the door and peeped out. He was just in time to see Philip return to the room.

When Philip had gone Jules joined his parents.

'Well, that went well.' He clapped his hands together appreciatively.

'You could have fooled us,' Peter said. 'Poor Philip seemed to be undergoing some esoteric sort of punishment, although I must admit I couldn't see a dunce's cap.'

'How so,' Jules said in astonishment. 'Oh I see. You spotted him outside the room with his hands on the wall.' He laughed.

Peter turned to Mary with an exaggerated look of innocence. 'Maniacal laughter do you think Mary.'

'Probably better than no laughter.' Mary glanced at Jules and smiled.

Jules explained what he had been doing and when he had finished all three rustled contentedly behind their papers.

Suddenly Jules's paper crackled excitedly. 'Listen to this. Whoever heard better.' Peter and Mary gazed across over the tops of their own, somewhat reluctantly lowered papers.

Jules read out, 'A Dr Norio Aoki in Japan has made a compact disc for cats and another for dogs.' Jules read on excitedly, put the paper down and turned to his parents.

'He's a vet and wanted to develop something to soothe the animals when they were brought to his surgery. He played different sorts of music to animals and recorded their reactions. He noted their ear movements and pupil sizes, he recorded their electrocardiograms and electroencephalograms and, good heavens, even X-rayed their colons. Then he took his results to a composer and they made the discs. Can you beat it? It jolly well shows the importance of music, doesn't it?'

'It certainly does, and I see, with great satisfaction, that you, Jules, seem to be sorting out your own problems,' Peter said.

'Yes. If I hadn't had to find things out for Philip I might not

140

have done so. I might just have let it slide.'

'I know,' Mary said quietly. 'And it was agony to see it. Especially in someone one loves.'

Jules got up from his chair and kissed his mother on the forehead. Then he held her hand and reached over to Peter and pulled them up and clasped their waists. Tears were not far away from all three.

19

Jules and Philip established a strong rapport over the next few weeks. Philip started to learn to play the piano and reached the stage of reading the score where he could turn the pages of music for Jules sufficiently reliably to accompany Jules to the recitals as his page turner.

Requests for performances burgeoned as Jules's renewed enthusiasm declared itself in his playing.

They both found their appreciation of the vibrations of instruments developing to an extent Jules would not have believed in his former state of mind and they learnt to tell when instruments were out of tune.

Jules still needed to be informed of the acoustics of the hall where he was to play and singing was a problem, but they each found that hearing aids tended to distort the sounds and preferred to do without them, at least when playing.

Ralph shared their delight and organised a concert at which both Jules and Philip were to perform in the Church Hall.

'It's wonderful,' he told Winifred for the umpteenth time.

'I know. You have told me; more than once.'

'Even twice?' Ralph peeked at his wife through his fingers. 'Perhaps thrice?'

The church concert was a great success and well attended. All Jules's friends were there, including Fiona and Boris.

After the performance they sought Jules out. The latter was gathering up his music in the vestry, having sent Philip off to bed. He looked up startled as Boris spoke.

'Well done Jules. I enjoyed your concert enormously.'

'So did I,' Fiona added.

Jules smiled with relief. 'I'm so glad you came Boris, and you too Fiona. After my last effort with you I wonder that you will speak to me.'

'Let's forget it. I mean that.'

Boris came over to Jules and grasped his arm and shook him gently. He smiled into Jules's face.

Jules acknowledged the sincerity. 'I can see that you do, you really do. That's wonderful Boris. I don't deserve it.'

'We artists must stick together. We're precious, sensitive creatures.'

Fiona went to the door and closed it.

'Don't bother,' Jules said.

'I thought the draught might knock over such sensitive creatures, I think those were the words you used.' Fiona roared with laughter and joined the others. 'But seriously Jules I was so pleased to hear you play and to see you so happy.' She gave him an affectionate peck on the cheek.

'Is that all I'm getting? With that build up I was looking for something more.'

'That's all you're getting,' said Boris. 'We've something to tell you. You're the first to know.'

A cloud passed over Jules's features and his eyelids widened. 'I can guess.'

'Go on then,' Boris said.

Jules took a deep breath and smiled. 'You're engaged.'

'Correct in one.'

Fiona still appeared a little anxious. She looked straight at Jules.

'We'll always be friends, won't we?' She smiled and touched his cheek lightly with her fingers. 'Dear Jules.'

'Very special friends.' They stood looking at each other.

'Hey, it's cold out here,' Boris exclaimed.

Jules grabbed Boris and they all stood together holding each other.

'It's great,' said Jules, 'just great.'

'I'm so glad.' Fiona smiled through tears she could not hold back.

☆ ☆ ☆

When she arrived home that evening Fiona was troubled. All the way back she had felt her feelings in turmoil. She thought she loved Boris but after her encounter that day with Jules she recognised a special feeling of belonging with him which she realised she did not feel towards Boris.

Marigold soon detected the little signals of distress and uncertainty which Fiona unconsciously was showing when she got in.

'Is anything troubling you dear?'

Marigold plonked herself on a kitchen chair and gestured to Fiona, who was standing morosely at the sink toying with a tea-towel, to sit down.

Fiona flung the towel on to the dresser and plumped down near her mother. She banged her elbows onto the table and clasped her face with her hands.

'I don't know, I can't decide something.'

'Something to do with boys no doubt, that's usually the problem with young girls of your age?' Marigold smiled and nudged Fiona's arm gently.

'Yes I suppose it is, well, it definitely is.' Fiona brought her arms down from her face and looked at her mother. 'You know I'm engaged to Boris?'

'Yes?'

'I thought I loved him, but how do I know? I've never been in love before?'

'Go on.'

'I met Jules today and told him. It seemed to stir up my feelings for him. I suppose I had tried to suppress them. I know your and Dad's feelings about it, the worry of his deafness and so on, especially in a musician, so that's probably why I had pushed under my feelings towards him. I realise now, or I think I do, that the feelings go rather deeper than I had thought. Oh, it's all a muddle in my mind.' She broke off and gave a huge sigh.

'It's very difficult for me to know just what to say.' Marigold looked serious and shook her head. 'My common sense says that to marry Jules would be, well, risky at the best and disastrous at the worst. It's all very well for a highfalutin' disregard for the practicalities of this life but after the first fine, careless rapture has worn off, and believe you me it will, the bills start to come in and have to be met. What's more, an artistic temperament is all very well somewhere else, but actually uncomfortable in one's own family.'

'But what about love, doesn't that count?' Fiona sounded indignant and frowned at her mother.

'Of course it matters. But doesn't that beg the question rather? Who do you love? There are different sorts of love and some of them don't last long, I can tell you. I can remember when you and Jules have been quite scratchy together, more than ever I recall with Boris.'

'Yes, you're right there Mum, but that might mean that my feelings for Jules are stronger. Oh, I don't know, I don't want to talk about it.'

Marigold burst out laughing at that and Gilbert appeared, sticking his head round the kitchen door.

'What's going on here?'

Marigold and Fiona both looked round. 'Girls' problems,' Fiona said.

'Well, I'm off then,' and he disappeared.

☆ ☆ ☆

Jules likewise was in turmoil. The prospect of losing Fiona to Boris aroused passions in him which he had not fully admitted before, like a puff of wind in the embers of a fire.

All next day his thoughts kept returning to Fiona and by the evening he could stand it no longer. Without telling his parents he slipped out of the house and set off to the Blakes'. He had only the vaguest idea of what he would do or say when he got there.

It was past suppertime when he arrived and he could see Fiona and her mother clearing away the supper things. It was getting dark and the lights had been switched on. Soon they disappeared, he presumed into the kitchen to wash up. Of Gilbert there was no sign and Jules supposed he was still in the garden.

146

He went up to the front door and rang the bell. He could hear footsteps and then Fiona opened the door.

'Jules,' she said putting her hand to her mouth. 'What are you doing here?'

'I must see you Fiona. May I?'

'Of course, come in,' she hesitated, 'or shall we go for a walk?'

'I'd much rather a walk; there are things I must say to you.'

'Just a minute while I fetch a jacket.' She left Jules at the porch and was back in an instant.

They walked off down the road, the streetlights giving each of them a yellow glow.

'I felt I had to see you Fiona, I can't let it go without seeing you.'

'I know, I don't mind Jules, it's not easy to sort out one's thoughts and feelings.' She stood under a street lamp so that Jules could read her lips.

'It's one thing to lose something, something precious, because you lose the battle. That can't be helped. But it's another thing, much worse, to lose something without trying, without struggling for it. I can't let that happen.' Jules looked hard at Fiona.

'Am I something precious? Thank you for that Jules. You are precious to me too, very precious.'

She broke off and they started walking again slowly. 'But I do love Boris. I don't know how I should explain it. It's a more steady love if you like, but one that I feel will grow. I love you too Jules, you must know that, but somehow I don't think it would last.'

Jules looked pained. 'Why not? Why wouldn't it last? What's wrong with me?' He broke off angrily.

'Oh, I know. It's my deafness isn't it? I'm not a good risk, not a reliable breadwinner? Tainted.' He spat the last word out.

'That's being silly Jules, it's not like that at all. That's nothing to do with it.' She hesitated. 'Well, I suppose it is in a way, but not in the bald, crude way you put it. If I loved you fully and without doubt, then I shouldn't care tuppence if you were deaf, or blind. It's because my love for you is, well not wholehearted I suppose, that these other matters come into the picture.' They

147

stood on the pavement, facing each other.

'Well, what if Boris were deaf?' Jules demanded. 'How would you feel about him then?'

Fiona was silent while she tried to sort out her thoughts.

'You see,' Jules went on, 'you're not sure.'

'I'm only waiting because I want to give you a fair reply, a truthful reply Jules, not one plucked off my cuff.'

Jules felt the force of her resentment. 'I'm sorry Fiona, but it means a lot to me.'

'And to me too, that's why I'm thinking hard before I reply. I feel, as a matter of fact, that your reaction just now gives me my answer. I would love Boris, even if he were deaf, because there's something solid about him that you haven't got. You're too up and down for me. Fine for an artist, hit the peaks and troughs and wail about it on your piano or in your sonnets, but a bit difficult to live with. There's your answer. I like you Jules, even love you at times perhaps, but I'm going to marry Boris and that's that.'

Jules stood still and regarded Fiona. He saw her determined little figure in the streetlights. He knew she was right, at least he had tried; honour was satisfied. 'All right Fiona, but we can always be good friends, can't we?'

'Certainly Jules, always.'

20

Philip's schooling improved markedly during these months, except for French. He had discarded his hearing aid altogether on Jules's advice, partly because it distorted the sounds during his music sessions and partly because he was trying to rely on lip-reading, facial expressions and bodily gestures.

The masters were playing their part in trying to remember to face the pupils while talking and all was going well other than the French.

One day Mrs Wilkins stopped Ralph and Jules in the street. 'Hello Vicar. Hello Mr Osk. Philip is doing fine apart from one thing.'

'What on earth's that?' Ralph enquired.

'French. He's still not managing French. And he loves French, or he used to.'

'How strange,' said Jules, 'he's never mentioned anything to me about that.'

'No. Well he doesn't want to upset you does he? He's so pleased with what you are doing Mr Osk. He doesn't like to seem ungrateful. You know how lads are.'

'Dear me,' said Ralph. 'I wonder who teaches him French?'

'Oh I know.' Mrs Wilkins tried to suppress her laughter with mixed results. A hearty chuckle turned into a spasmodic cough.

'Do you smoke?' said Ralph sternly. 'I rather feel you do.'

'Well, now and then Vicar. You know.'

'What I do know is that you would be well advised to stop it. That's what I know. Don't you agree Jules?'

'I'm afraid I do Mrs Wilkins. But why did you laugh?'

'Because it's the Headmaster who teaches our Philip his French. And he prides himself on it what's more, that I do know.' Mrs Wilkins paused for her information to sink in.

'Oh dear. That does make it a bit awkward. But if he is such a good teacher why is Philip doing so badly?'

'I think I've got it.' Jules suddenly brightened up. 'Has he a beard Mrs Wilkins?'

'What, Mr Brewster? He certainly has, a massive great black thing, all over his face. He's very proud of it, I believe.'

'What are you driving at Jules?' Ralph looked on puzzled.

'Don't you see. Philip is depending a lot on lip movements and facial expressions to hear his teachers. The beard obscures all that.'

'Good heavens.' Ralph clapped his hands with delight. 'Who would ever have thought of that?'

'So that's it,' said Mrs Wilkins thoughtfully.

'You seem to be pondering something Mrs Wilkins. Out with it.' Ralph went nearer to her.

'Well,' said Mrs Wilkins hesitantly, 'there is a solution.'

'And I've just thought of it,' said Jules, 'and you can count me out.' He pretended to walk away.

'Hey where are you going Jules?' said Ralph, 'You can't leave me in the lurch. I haven't twigged the answer yet and I'm supposed to be intelligent.'

Ralph cupped his chin in the palm of his hand and closed his eyes. Suddenly he opened them with a look of horror. The other two laughed.

'You're the one to do it,' Jules teased. 'I've seen you in action on the toenails. Now's the opportunity to extend your repertoire.'

'That's right,' Mrs Wilkins added helpfully.

'Opportunity's not the only thing which is knocking. Look at my knees.'

'We'd rather not if you don't mind.'

'I happen to know that Mr Brewster is not one to be easily trifled with. Does he have any weak spots I wonder? Oh dear, I don't think I can face up to it. Ask him to shave off his beloved beard. Oh dear.' Ralph quailed.

'We must do it,' Jules said decisively. 'We must beard him in his den.'

'You mean de-beard him; den retreat, don't you?' Ralph perked up at this sally.

'You two. I'm going to leave you to it.'

'In it's more the mark Mrs Wilkins,' said Ralph. 'But we'll do our best, I promise you.'

'I wish I could be there,' said Mrs Wilkins as she set off.

Ralph was sure he heard a chuckle from her before she disappeared.

The two men stood irresolute on the pavement. Fletcher saw them as he cycled past.

'Pretending to be Lot's wives, are we?' he shouted.

'He only had one wife,' Ralph shouted back. 'I'm a pillar of strength, not a pillar of salt.'

'Right, that's it Ralph, I heard that,' Jules exclaimed. 'You will have to confront Mr Brewster right now, after that boast.'

Ralph groaned. 'I suppose so. Come on then. The sooner the better.'

☆ ☆ ☆

Afternoon school had finished and the pair found Mr Brewster in his study. He was a big man, with a large black beard, luxuriant eyebrows and a paunch to match. He did not seem to be in the best of humour.

'What can I do for you two? Come begging for something I'll be bound. Sit down.'

Ralph cleared his throat, which had become dry.

'Er. You know Philip, Mr Brewster, Philip Wilkins.'

'Yes, of course I do. The deaf boy.'

'Well,' Ralph hesitated and took the plunge, 'he's doing well in all his classes except for French.'

'And I teach him French. What, pray, are you implying from that? That I am incompetent? How dare you.'

Mr Brewster rose from his desk and strode up and down the room. After hesitating, Ralph got up and followed the Head's movements like a timorous doppelganger.

151

'Stop shadowing me Vicar, for goodness sake. Do sit down. You don't really think I am a bad teacher do you?'

Mr Brewster paused and looked enquiringly at each of the others in turn.

'It's not that, it's your beard.'

'My beard. How on earth can you blame my beard? It doesn't do the teaching. It is there for ornament, not teaching.'

Mr Brewster surveyed his beard in a small wall mirror with satisfaction and stroked it tenderly.

'Don't you see,' said Ralph desperately, 'your beard stops young Philip from seeing your facial expressions and your lip movements. It's hard enough anyway with a foreign tongue and that's what the problem is.'

Ralph sat back and drew a deep breath which he slowly released as he glanced at Jules.

'That's it,' Jules added helpfully. 'I am deaf myself and I am trying to get Philip to rely more on lip-reading and facial expressions than on a hearing aid.'

Mr Brewster started to speak slowly and thoughtfully. 'I cannot give him another French teacher without disrupting an entire class. He's a good lad Philip. Doing well in school recently. Vast improvement in fact. I'll do it by God!'

'You mean you'll shave off your beard just to help Philip?' Ralph danced across the floor to him. 'You're a brick.'

'We've just been pillars of salt and now you're a brick Mr Brewster. We should do well together.' Jules got up to join Ralph.

'You don't look like pillars of salt to me,' said Mr Brewster. Jules explained.

'It's the most Christian act I have come across for some time. I appreciate what it must cost you.' Ralph stopped with a sudden inspiration. 'You know I am always on the lookout for fund-raising activities for the Church.'

'Oh no,' said Mr Brewster emphatically. 'I am not going to have it done outside your church as a spectacle to raise money. That's going too far.'

'Yes it is Ralph, really,' Jules added.

'I suppose you're right,' Ralph said regretfully. 'Who shall do

152

the deed then?'

'My barber,' said Mr Brewster firmly.

'Could we guess the weight?' Ralph asked hopefully.

Mr Brewster eyed him sharply. 'What? The weight of my beard, the trimmings? Oh I suppose so. You're incorrigible Vicar. Quite incorrigible.'

'Ah, but irresistible, that too, wouldn't you say?'

'I think we might.' Mr Brewster looked across at Jules for support.

'We might indeed. Ralph has a way.' Jules laughed.

'Well, our way is out right now. Come on Jules. Thanks a million Mr Brewster.' Ralph waved airily. 'Come on Jules, no dilly-dallying.'

☆ ☆ ☆

It was only when he approached home that Giles Brewster appreciated the full enormity of his undertaking.

His wife Patricia was one of these ageless women with straight hair and a determination to match. Her slightly bowed figure contrasted with an unbowed, and some said unbowable, will-power, forged in the crucible of the Women's Institute and such-like stalwart associations of womenfolk.

Mr Brewster entered hesitantly. 'Have a good day, dear?' He poked at her cheek with his lips.

'When you seem so, what shall I say, so submissive, I suspect something Giles.'

'Oh no Patricia. Nothing really.' Giles glanced regretfully in the mirror.

'What are you gawping at? Haven't you seen yourself before?'

Giles pondered desperately whether to present his case as a decision on his own part or whether to enlarge on the philanthropic aspect. He wondered which alternative would be best received.

'Sometimes we have to do things we don't want to do,' he said enigmatically.

'Have you wiped your shoes?' Patricia glanced at his feet.

'It's rather the other end.'

'Well, have you wiped your nose then?'

'No. It's none of those things. Something much more important I have to do. *"Dulce et decorum est".*' He gave a wistful smile and let it linger.

Patricia eyed him shrewdly. 'This is something quite important, isn't it? I feel a heaviness in the air. Out with it.'

'Off with it would be more the mark actually.'

'Off with his head. Surely not that Giles? No wonder you were muttering that ridiculous Latin tag. Oh come on, for goodness sake, let's get it over with. What are you up to?'

Giles gulped. 'I'm going to have my beard shaved off.' He paused to let the news sink in.

Patricia sat down suddenly. 'You can't. Look what happened to Samson. I shall leave you if you do.'

'Is that a promise or a threat? No, I didn't mean that.'

Giles rushed over and pretended to sit on Patricia's lap. He thrust his beard towards her.

'Get away you hairy creature. You're tickling me.'

'We can have porridge then for breakfast, and you know how you like that.'

Patricia shuddered.

'With salt.'

'Oh stop it. This is serious. What on earth has occasioned this extraordinary decision on your part and why was I not consulted about it?'

'Because,' Giles rose and assumed a majestic pose, 'because a man's got to do what a man's got to do.'

'Very clear, I'm sure. I forbid it.' She snapped her lips together.

'Very well. You will have the whole community on your heels if you do.'

'Why. I'm not running a race?'

'You know of Philip Wilkins?'

'What? The deaf boy. He's doing so well now, isn't he?'

'Apart from French. And who teaches him French?'

'You do. But I still don't see.'

Giles explained.

When he had finished Patricia came over and hugged him.

Her eyes were glowing.

'I think that's the most wonderful thing and I know what it's cost you. I'm proud of you. I really am dear.'

Mr Brewster was as good as his word. His barber carefully shaved him with hands trembling at the enormity of his task, and kept the shavings for weighing. Gasps of astonishment greeted Mr Brewster's entrance at assembly two days later. News of the impending transformation had trickled through, and as he started to address the school a thunderous cheering and clapping arose, accompanied by stamping of feet on the floor, and continued for some time. Mr Brewster stood there and tried to hide his tears.

21

Bernard Wilkins scowled out of his front room window. 'Drat the boy. Where is he?'

Rhona joined him and peered out. They made a stolid pair. Bernard wore a vest, through and behind which his muscular frame proclaimed itself emphatically. Rhona's unkempt hair tickled his shoulder as she craned her neck towards the window.

'You're tickling me girl.' Bernard hoisted her by the waist and plonked her down in his arms. He gave her a bear hug and buried his face in her hair. His nose snagged a hairpin on its journey.

'Good God woman. What's that in your hair. Barbed wire or something?'

'Got to have some protection to fend you off.'

They heard the sound of voices outside and saw Philip and Jules standing there. Each was intently watching the other's lips and conversation flowed unimpeded.

'What are they chattering about?' Bernard growled. 'I'm hungry for my tea.'

'Philip has got on well with Mr Osk's help, Bernie. Even his French is picking up since Mr Brewster shaved his beard off.'

Bernard guffawed and went to open the front door. 'Come on Philip,' he bellowed. 'You can't stay there all night.'

Philip saw him and the animation left his face. 'I must go Jules. See you.'

When they were having their tea Bernard's irritation gathered strength. Signs of its presence multiplied; he banged his cup into the saucer, leaving it slewed. His thick arm moved imperiously

157

as it gathered food. He was silent. Rhona and Philip waited, the
other children deserting for the television.

'You seem very friendly with that young fellow, what's his
name? Jules Osk. What a prissy name. I should be careful
young lad if I were you.'

'Oh Bernie,' Rhona exclaimed. 'What on earth are you
driving at? There's nothing like that, I'm sure.'

'How do you know? From what you read in the papers these
days it's all too likely.' Bernard scowled ominously at Philip.

'He's helped me a lot Dad. I probably wouldn't be able to
hear what you're saying now if it weren't for him.'

'Well then I'll speak louder. He isn't the only one who helps
you.'

'Bernie, you'll upset the lad. Shut up.'

'I'll not be shut up in my own home, buggered if I will.'

'Don't swear like that Bernard. Especially in front of the boy.'

'It's about time he got to know about words like that.'

Rhona stood up. 'You be careful with your filthy language.
Keep your stinking thoughts to yourself.'

Philip's distress boiled over and he ran to his bedroom and
slammed the door.

'Now look what you've done. Upset the boy.'

'Better upset now, like this, than something worse later.'
Bernard strode out to his garden.

Rhona sighed as she started to clear the table. When she had
finished she knocked on Philip's door and tried the handle. It
was locked. She shrugged and went back to the kitchen.

☆　☆　☆

Philip lay on his bed. He knew what his father had been hinting
at and was horrified. His affection for Jules had become strong
and now it felt tainted, like a beautiful portrait on which
someone had daubed an obscene mark. He shuddered and
turned over on the bed.

It was nearly midnight and he had not yet undressed. Was his
love of Jules like his father had hinted? Buggery. He had heard
gossip at school about such things with sniggers and winks, like

158

all his pals. Now it didn't seem so funny. Why did he like Jules so much? Was it normal or was he abnormal? Philip's thoughts jostled about in his mind and he became more and more upset.

He lay on his back on his bed and regarded the shadow patterns cast on the ceiling by the street lamp outside. He had not drawn his curtains and the branches of a tree waved as if sniggering and laughing at him. What did he know about nature, they seemed to be saying? We've seen it all.

He got up and tiptoed to the door. Carefully he opened it. A feeling of revulsion came over him. He closed his door quietly and went downstairs. He went to the back door, unlocked' it and slid outside noiselessly.

The sky was a rich, deep blue, studded with stars, and a half moon beamed his way to the road and beyond. His trainers were soundless as he hurried along. He climbed over a gate and made towards the coppice. The grass was wet and felt cold as he swished along. When he looked back the footprints left dark marks where the grass was crushed. He had an impulse to bury himself in the wood to drown out the vile insinuations his father had made. Although he knew them to be without foundation yet they still rankled in his mind and seemed to contaminate his thoughts.

He scrambled through the hedge, cutting his hands in the process, and his windcheater caught on a bramble and tore when he tugged to release it. He plunged deeper into the wood and did not notice a branch which smote his cheek and brought tears to his eyes. A disturbed blackbird yaffled in alarm but he did not hear it as he plunged to the ground and sobbed.

22

The next morning Fletcher Pemberton was up bright and early as usual. He sniffed the fresh morning air and his rubicund face glowed. He surveyed the day and cocked his ear at the birds. The morning chorus had faded to a scattered comment on the day and its possibilities.

Suddenly Fletcher heard an unusual fusillade of calls from the old coppice.

I wonder if that old fox is late back to his lair? He set off to investigate. He entered the wood stealthily and paused to listen but everything had gone silent.

Philip, who had been shivering, unable to sleep, and lacking the willpower to move, heard nothing. He lay among the leaves, which he had tried to burrow under for shelter, and pondered what he should do. He pulled himself up with the aid of an overhanging branch and it cracked.

Fletcher heard the sound and tensed. He stole forward and parted some branches which were in his way. Then he saw Philip, half hidden under the leaves and branches.

'Philip. What are you doing here?'

Philip saw him with a start and half comprehended what he was saying.

He smiled sheepishly. 'Hello Mr Pemberton. Did I startle you?'

'You certainly did. What's wrong?' Fletcher noted the tear-stained face and bedraggled condition.

'I can't tell you Mr Pemberton. Something upset me. I'm sorry. I ought to go home.'

'You certainly ought. Let's go together. I'll see you to your house and leave you there.'

When they reached their destination Philip glanced anxiously at his parents' bedroom window. The curtains were drawn back. He hesitated.

'Now in you go Philip. Better come clean to your parents. It's always wiser in the long run.'

Philip grinned sheepishly. 'Thanks Mr Pemberton.' He disappeared round to the back of the house.

His mother's head could be seen through the kitchen window. She was washing some dishes at the sink when he opened the back door and entered. He stood in the centre of the kitchen with his gaze on the floor, uncertain what to do.

Rhona looked at him, her hands motionless, still holding the dishcloth and a plate which steamed in the sunlight from the window.

'Well,' she said slowly so that he could see her lips. 'and where have you been? You had us worried. Dad is getting ready to go down to the police station. Dad,' she shouted up the stairs, 'he's here.'

'What's that you say?' Bernard bellowed down from the landing. 'Is that Philip you've got?'

'Yes. He's just come in.'

Heavy footfalls were heard as Bernard hurried down the stairs. He came into the kitchen, holding his unfastened trousers with one hand and trying vainly to button up his shirt with the other.

'Now then you young tyke. Where the hell have you been?'

Philip was silent.

'Speak up, I tell you. You've enough to say when you're with him.'

'Oh don't Bernard. Leave the lad alone. Can't you see he's been upset?'

Rhona went over and drew Philip to her. He flung his arms round her waist.

Bernard was furious. He swung Philip round by his shoulder and tore him from Rhona.

'I won't have sullenness. You listen to me. Where the hell have you, been?'

'I went out. In the woods.'

'What the hell for? You look a bloody mess. Go and get washed and tidy yourself up. How long were you out?'

'Dunno. Can't remember.' Philip clasped his mother again.

'Let him be Bernie. Run along Philip and tidy yourself up.'

When they heard Philip enter his room Rhona turned to her husband.

'I think he's been out most of the night, poor lad. Lay off him. There's probably nothing in what you say anyway. Can't men and boys be friends any more without all this, this innuendo?'

'Innuendo is it? You've been reading too many books, or more likely women's magazines.'

'Well anyway he's had enough.'

'All right,' Bernard muttered ungraciously. 'But I shall be watching, mind you.'

'Mind you don't see what isn't there.'

☆ ☆ ☆

Over the next few weeks Jules thought he detected a change in Philip's responsiveness to him. When Jules offered him a friendly dig Philip backed away and at the end of the lessons he hurried off with a variety of excuses.

He mentioned it to Ralph one day. 'I can't make it out. He was so friendly and natural but in the last few weeks he's behaved as if he were frightened of me, almost shrinking from me I would have said.'

Ralph nodded sagely. 'It's a complicated world Jules. You know that.'

'And what do you precisely mean by that Ralph? The Delphic utterance doesn't become you. You're more of a "trot it out and let's face it" sort of chap.'

Ralph grinned and swept his hands over his temples with no apparent effect on the unruly locks. 'I think I know my parishioners well enough to surmise what has happened.'

'Well out with it then. It's not like you to bottle it up.'

'No. But there are times when the truth, or rather the sus-

163

pected truth, is better bottled up than battled with.'

'I am beginning to guess the general trend.' Jules blushed. 'And I don't like it, not one little bit. And it's not true, what's more. You believe that, I hope, don't you Ralph?'

'Yes I do. I've a good mind to tackle Bernard Wilkins about it,' Ralph said slowly.

'But will it do any good?'

'It might help Philip. I'll see.'

23

The friendship of the Pemberton and Blake families prospered and they arranged to join in a coach trip to London; the wives to go their way and the husbands theirs.

'At least they won't be able to pursue their usual nature studies,' Marigold said to Doris.

'That's what I'm worried about,' Doris retorted, and they both pealed with laughter.

'What on earth are you two girls cackling about?' Fletcher asked.

'Never you mind,' they replied in unison.

☆ ☆ ☆

On the day of the outing Doris and Marigold were soon swallowed up among the crowd in Oxford Street. Fletcher and Gilbert stood at the tube entrance.

'I've a notion,' Fletcher whispered conspiratorially to Gilbert. 'You know my old pig Sniffer.'

'Intimately.'

'Well, he's got me interested in smells in general.'

'You haven't hidden him in the coach, have you Fletch? As a sort of bet, to see who would spot him, or smell him?'

'No I have not. It would have been an idea though. We could have seen what he made of London smells. No, but it's to do with smells. Have a guess.'

'I guess . . .' Gilbert pondered. 'I guess, oh I don't know, we're going to Billingsgate Market.'

'It's moved, hasn't it? But what a notion. Sniffer would have gone wild. Another time perhaps.' Fletcher sighed regretfully. 'No. Have you heard of aromatherapy? I've got interested in that.'

'I think I've heard of it. Didn't a well know politician and some of the royals get interested in it? A look of suspicion appeared on Gilbert's face and he tugged at his moustache. 'You're not suggesting that we have aromatherapy are you?'

'Well, not exactly. But I am suggesting we sniff it out, as you might say. Go and have a look. I've got an address here.' Fletcher pulled out a clip from a newspaper.

Gilbert sighed. 'All right then.'

They descended the stairs of the tube station and made their way to Kensington. It did not take them long to find their destination. The Sandalwood Clinic for Aches and Pains was situated in a dingy side street off Kensington High Street. It's modest proclamation of intent over the lintel of the narrow doorway, 'To Soothe and Relax', contrasted with the more flamboyant notices nearby, displaying such important matters as 'Sex Therapist to the Establishment', 'A Week in Bangkok with Up-and-Coming Tours', 'Lumbago Relieved' and 'Clairvoyance for Racing Punters'.

'Here we are,' Fletcher said firmly. He strode down a flight of rickety stairs which echoed and groaned with every step.

Gilbert contemplated flight.

'Come on man,' Fletcher said sternly.

Gilbert shrugged his shoulders and descended slowly. Fletcher rang a bell on a door with frosted glass panels. They waited. A giggle was heard, then rapid footfalls. The door opened and a young man's head appeared. He had a pointed, olive-complexioned face with short black hair, fringed over the forehead. His dark eyes darted from Fletcher to Gilbert.

'Oh hello,' he said. 'Have you come about the aromatherapy?' He spoke rapidly.

'That's it,' said Fletcher, 'I saw your advert in the paper.'

By this time a strong herbal aroma had reached them in the passage. 'I'm Martyn Sandalwood. Come in.'

Martyn ushered them through a small front office where a

girl was sitting at a desk. She wore a gown of many hues, large earrings dangled each side of her neck and she had abundant, untidy fair hair.

'This is Floria, my secretary.'

They passed into a central room with a single light bulb hanging from the low ceiling. From the doors on each side there emanated strong perfumes. Moisture glistened on the white walls and an extractor fan grappled gamely with the vapours.

Martyn drew up two wooden chairs and invited the men to be seated. He perched himself on the side of a table and kept getting up with nimble movements to pace up and down in the confined space.

'You are aware of aromatherapy I take it, or you wouldn't be here.'

'I am,' said Fletcher. 'My friend and I were in London and thought we would find out more about it, isn't that so Gilbert?'

'Ooooo you naughty things.' Martyn gave them a wink.

'That's right,' Gilbert replied in his gruffest voice. He tensed the masseter muscles on his face and frowned.

'Shall I give you a quick rundown as to what we have and then you can choose what you need.'

Martyn opened a large cupboard to reveal several rows of different coloured bottles, some clean and pristine, others marked with trickles and stains. The scents wafted across the room. Martyn breathed in deeply and glanced towards the ceiling.

'Wonderful,' he said. He seized a bottle. 'They all contain essential oils. They are the substances which do the trick. Do you know what an essential oil is?'

'Sort of,' Fletcher answered. 'The smelly part.'

'Quite so. The definition of an essential oil is an odorous and volatile substance obtained by a physical process from a natural source of a single species. That's pretty good for an arts graduate don't you think?'

'How did you get interested in it?' Gilbert enquired.

'Muscular tension my dear man. And headaches. Smell this.'

He advanced, unscrewed the stopper and thrust the neck of a bottle under their noses.

Fletcher and Gilbert made tentative sniffs and then inhaled more deeply.

'What do you get?' Martyn demanded.

'Forests and fragrance,' Fletcher replied. He sat back in his chair. 'Very relaxing.'

'Absolutely. It is, in fact, my patronymic, sandalwood. Very good to alleviate stress. If it's muscular relaxation you want then marjoram is your man. The right amount relaxes, too much paralyses. That's where the expertise comes in. What do you gentlemen feel you need?'

'I'd like to try something', said Fletcher, 'now that we're here. Wouldn't you Gilbert?'

Gilbert looked doubtful. 'I suppose so. What do you charge?'

'If you just want an aroma massage, it's thirty five pounds.'

Fletcher and Gilbert hesitated. 'Oh come on,' said Fletcher. 'Now we're here. Think what the girls will be spending in Oxford Street.'

'All right,' said Gilbert. 'I'm game.'

'An excellent idea.' Martyn shouted through to Floria 'Two oil massages. Can you come and give one.' He turned back to Fletcher and Gilbert. 'How about a nice lavender oil massage for you?' He indicated Fletcher, 'and I'll give your friend a going-over with sandalwood.'

Half an hour later Fletcher and Gilbert emerged onto the street.

Two young girls passing by giggled and they heard one say to the other 'Phew. You meet all sorts in London. Did you smell them?'

The girls glanced back and laughed more loudly. Fletcher and Gilbert grew uneasy as they noticed the varied reactions of the passers-by.

'Oh crumbs,' Gilbert exclaimed. 'I think we smell a bit.'

'You're right. I think we do, but I feel very relaxed about it.'

'You may do,' said Gilbert tersely. 'You don't smell as much as I do. That lavender oil was pretty potent. Oh crikey. What are the girls going to say?'

Fletcher glanced at his watch. 'We'll soon find out. It's time we rejoined the coach.'

They spotted the coach just off Smith Square. It was fairly full and several people were gossiping at the entrance. They walked along outside and saw their wives in their seats.

The girls waved at the menfolk through steamy windows. 'Come on in,' they mouthed.

'Now for it,' Gilbert said with resignation. 'We'd better take a deep breath and get on.'

'As long as all the others don't take deep breaths, that's what I'm worried about,' Fletcher laughed. 'Let's put our mackintoshes on. It might help to mask things.' They donned their macs and climbed aboard.

'Expecting rain are we?' said a wag near the front. They reached their wives.

'What on earth have you got your mac on for?' Marigold demanded.

Gilbert looked sheepish and glanced to Fletcher for help. Fletcher gave a faint shrug and left Gilbert to it.

'We got a bit chilly dear.'

'Well you don't look chilly. In fact you look extremely hot, and glistening. You've got a glistening sort of look. Oily. What have you two been up to? For goodness sake take that mac off. You'll get heatstroke in here. Look how the windows are steamed up.'

'Yes, I agree Marigold,' Doris chipped in. 'For goodness sake take those macs off.'

Fletcher and Gilbert exchanged the kind of comradely glance which parachutists give while they wait to jump and then unbuttoned their macs. They looked at each other and, with perfect timing, swung their arms wide and pulled the macs off.

At once a powerful aroma of lavender oil and sandalwood pervaded the bus, having been pent up behind the macs and now making up for lost time.

Looks of mingled incredulity and mirth spread down the coach like a Mexican wave.

'What on earth have you two been up to?' Doris exclaimed. 'You both smell like, like gigolos.'

'Or pansies,' shouted someone else.

'Give us a kiss,' shouted another. The ribaldry spread.

Fletcher and Gilbert stood in the aisle speechless.

Suddenly Fletcher brightened up. 'Come on Gilbert. Let's give them their money's worth.'

He placed the back of his right hand across his hip and held the left delicately before him, the fingers drooping and slightly apart and flounced down the aisle. Gilbert looked with desperation at Marigold.

'Come on Gilbert. Don't let your friend down,' Marigold shouted, laughing unrestrainedly. 'Off you go.'

Gilbert attempted to ape Fletcher and pursued him desperately.

Applause broke out from the coach party and one or two started to sing 'Greenery yallery, Grosvenor Gallery, foot in the grave your man.'

Others joined in, 'Francesca di Rimini, niminy, piminy, je ne sais quoi young man.'

A large man with a loud voice then drowned them all out with a rendering of 'I'm called little Buttercup-dear little Buttercup. Though I could never tell why.'

Fletcher and Gilbert reached the door and hesitated.

The driver grinned. 'No you don't,' and firmly closed the doors which swung to with a thud of finality which the two saw with dismay.

They turned and faced their companions. Suddenly a thought occurred to Gilbert.

He whispered above the din to Fletcher. 'Hey Fletch, I've got an idea. Let them all draw lots for their seats on the coach. We'll number bits of paper and number one can choose how far or how near they sit to us and so on. We'll sit at the back I think, don't you?'

'Brilliant,' Fletcher beamed, 'we can keep an eye on things from there. Let 'em have the good news Gilbert old man.'

They waved their arms for silence and the din slowly subsided.

'Since we are so appreciated,' Gilbert said loudly, 'we have decided you must all draw lots to see who sits next to us on the journey back. Don't get hurt in the stampede.'

'We'll put pieces of paper with numbers on them in a hat, starting at number one.'

'Are you sure you've got that right?' someone shouted.

He received a withering glance from Gilbert and Fletcher.

The numbers were written out on pieces of paper and the coach driver's hat purloined for the receptacle. The draw was made with much commotion.

'Now then,' shouted Fletcher above the hubbub, 'who's the lucky one with number one?'

'I have,' said a large lady with a floral hat, 'and I wish to be seated as far away as possible from you two, from you two precious objects. If you are sitting at the back then I shall sit here.' And she decisively plonked herself down on one of the front seats.

The others all joined in the game and the coach at last set off.

'When we get home I shall pack Gilbert off to have a bath at once,' said Marigold.

'So shall I,' said Doris, 'pronto.'

24

Ralph pondered on Jules's and Philip's friendship. He was convinced it was a perfectly normal one and felt that Philip's father had probably been the cause of his son's apparent wariness of manner towards Jules.

He decided it was his obligation to tackle Mr Wilkins on the matter, conjectural though it all was.

The next evening he called at the Wilkins' house at a time when he knew Philip was having a music lesson with Jules.

Mrs Wilkins answered the door, still drying her hands and showing a fleck of pastry on one cheek.

'Oh it's you Mr Dene,' She stood there. 'I am afraid we are not much of churchgoers.'

She blushed and brushed the pastry crumbs off her cheek with a flick of the finger. 'You've caught us napping a bit.' She laughed.

'No I haven't come about your churchgoing or rather not going. That can wait for another time. I would like to have a word with your husband if I may.'

'Who's that?' Mr Wilkins's voice called from the kitchen.

There was the scraping of a chair.

'It's the vicar, Mr Dene. He wants a word with you,' said Mrs Wilkins.

'Oh does he.' Mr Wilkins voice became louder as he came to the front door.

His jaws were still chewing. 'Hello Vicar. Sorry about this but a man has to eat.'

'I know,' said Ralph. 'Have I come at a bad time?'

'No. Come on in Vicar,' Mrs Wilkins said. 'Let's shut the door and keep the cold out.'

Mr Wilkins looked regretfully at the warm kitchen whose light could be seen shining into the hall.

'Better come along in here Vicar.' He threw open his sitting-room door and put the light on.

Ralph saw a cold-looking room. 'The kitchen will be fine for me.'

'It's a real mess Vicar,' Mrs Wilkins said hurriedly. 'We've barely finished supper. Philip has his later.'

'It's warmth or decorum, take your choice Vicar. I know which I'd rather choose.'

'So do I,' said Ralph. They both moved rapidly into the kitchen before Mrs Wilkins could prevent them.

Mrs Wilkins launched herself at the table and cleared it while the men stood.

'Out of my way Bernie,' she expostulated.

'I think we'd better stand in the corner until Mrs Wilkins has finished,' Ralph said.

'Don't mind her. Have a cup of tea Vicar.'

Mr Wilkins moved towards the pot which had not yet been cleared but was cut off by a determined Mrs Wilkins.

'You can't offer the vicar that stale tea. I'll make you both a nice fresh pot.'

At last Mrs Wilkins was satisfied and the two men sat down.

'Now what is it you want to say Vicar?'

Ralph noticed the heavy, square features of the man opposite to him, the flushed cheeks and hazel eyes. The hair was cropped and stood up from the scalp like a stubble. The eyebrows seemed to have given up and vanished.

'I've come about the way Jules Osk is helping your Philip, Mr Wilkins.'

Ralph placed his hands on the table and looked straight at Mr Wilkins.

'Call me Bernard, Vicar.'

'Thank you, Bernard then. There seems to have been a change in Philip's attitude to Mr Osk. Jules has noticed it and so have I. They were getting on so well and Philip's learning

174

and enjoyment of life, I may say, were coming on apace, both at school and his music. Then all of a sudden he seemed to withdraw into himself. He's not doing so well now and rushes off as soon as he can, whereas before Jules could hardly get rid of him.'

Ralph paused. Bernard betrayed no emotion. Rhona had come to stand in the doorway from the larder with a tea-cloth hanging from her hand.

'So what do you think has happened?' Bernard said slowly.

There was silence. Rhona shuffled uneasily and resumed her drying up.

'I don't know what has happened, but something has.' Ralph was determined to go on, even without any help. 'I think myself that someone has been making suggestions, unpleasant suggestions.'

'Oh!' Bernard scowled and the flush in his cheeks heightened. His eyelids narrowed. 'What sort of unpleasant suggestions I wonder?'

'So do I Bernard. So do I.'

There was another pause. They were like two alley cats sniffing each other out, backs arched and tails on the twitch.

'I think someone may have suggested to Philip that there's something unhealthy in his friendship with Jules and it's made him wary.' Ralph said this quickly but with determination and watched Bernard's face.

'And what if there is eh? What if there is? How about it Vicar? You would know with your public school education, wouldn't you?'

It was Ralph's turn for his eyes to blaze. He clasped his hands together on the table and his skin blanched from the pressure. Rhona had paused to listen again.

'What do you mean by that Bernard? For one thing I didn't go to a public school but even if I had it doesn't mean I would be homosexual. That's what you're suggesting isn't it?'

'You raised the whole subject Vicar.'

'I raised the subject for the very good reason that I think someone has put such ideas into Philip's head and, what's more, I think that person is you.'

Ralph leant back in his chair and withdrew his hands from the table.

'And if I have, what of it? Maybe there's something in it. How should I know?'

Ralph leant forward again. 'For a start there's nothing in it and secondly it's having a bad effect on Philip.'

'He's my son and I'll tell him what I bloody well like. I don't want him caught up with you namby-pamby lot with your fine manners. All show.'

'Fine manners never did any harm. A little more politeness in this world would be welcome instead of all this "I'm all right Jack" attitude.'

'So that's what you think of the likes of us lot is it? Good for nothing except hard work. Sweat our guts out for you lot.'

Bernard angrily pushed his chair aside and stood up, leaning over the table.

Ralph felt the steel enter into him which he had come to recognise as part of his make-up when put under pressure. He had first noticed it at school when he had been bullied. Instead of giving in to the bully-boys he had been surprised and, in the end, gratified to find himself defying them with an implacable determination which produced the result, astonishing both to himself and to his antagonists, of his being left unmolested. Then a temptation which Ralph had found harder to resist rose up. When the bullies invited him to join them Ralph found he was better able to resist hostility than to resist offers of friendship. Over the years he had come to recognise such blandishments of flattery as more insidious so far as he was concerned.

Ralph slowly stood up and faced Bernard. 'It is rather typical of your type to resort to violence. I might have known it. I wonder whether you threaten Philip in that way at times? When he crosses you perhaps?'

'You're just about accusing me of assaulting my own child.' Bernard was furious. 'You silly little prig. Get out of my house.'

'I shall go in my own good time.' Ralph stood in front of his chair.

Bernard pushed him in the direction of the door but Ralph

stumbled over the chair and fell, hitting the side of his forehead on the table edge.

He struggled up and dabbed his handkerchief to the wound.

Rhona went to him with a damp cloth. 'Hold this on Vicar.'

Ralph stood pressing the cloth to the sore spot for a few moments, looking steadily at Bernard as he did so.

'Philip is what it is all about Bernard. You can't really think there is anything other than friendship between your Philip and Jules can you?'

'I dunno,' Bernard flopped into his chair. 'I'm sorry Vicar, I really am.'

'Well, what are you two going to say to Philip?' Rhona demanded. 'He'll be home soon.'

'Yes, what are we?' Ralph looked earnestly at Bernard. 'We've got to set the poor lad's mind at rest, and Jules's come to that.'

'Let's say,' said Bernard slowly, 'that we are glad Mr Osk is trying to help him.'

'Is that all? That won't do. You must say more than that, surely.'

'Well, what do you suggest Vicar? I'm not a dab hand at words like you.'

'I would say to him that you did not want to suggest there was anything improper in his friendship with Mr Osk but just wanted to make him aware of things. Something like that.'

'OK Vicar. I'll do that. Thank you for coming. I'm sorry about the bruise.'

'I've had worse. All in the line of duty. Goodbye Rhona, goodbye Bernard. Don't forget to speak to Philip now.'

25

Philip's piano playing improved steadily under Jules's tuition and his percussion made great bounds. He rejoiced to accompany Jules's piano playing with his own percussion instruments, the range of his rhythms continually extending. He seemed to sense when to be soft, so as not to drown out the piano, and he kept in perfect time, always preferring to keep Jules in his view if he could.

'I think we need a bass player, Philip, to complete the rhythm section.'

'Great,' said Philip.

'We'll find out if there is anyone suitable at school.'

A boy of sixteen called Frank Keighley was enlisted.

He was nearly as tall as his instrument and his podgy face, with its thick lips and floppy ears, would bob enthusiastically as he twanged away on the strings. He was affable and seemed quite content to maintain a steady pulse in the background while the other two trilled and rolled.

Ralph listened to their playing and was filled with enthusiasm.

When they had finished the piece they were playing in the church hall Ralph leapt from his chair and clapped his hands enthusiastically. 'Bravo the lot of you. You are ready to face your public.'

'Ah but are the public ready to face us, that's the question?' Jules said laughing.

'As ready as they'll ever be. I shall arrange a concert in this very hall. How long shall we say?'

'About half an hour should be long enough.'

'No, no, Jules dear boy. I mean how long till you are ready to perform. Shall we say next month?'

Jules consulted with the others and Ralph noted with amusement the looks of horror which appeared on their faces.

Eventually a date in six weeks time was decided upon.

Ralph was in high spirits and invited Jules back home to discuss the concert further. It was just getting dusk on an early summer evening as they swung in at the vicarage gate. The house was unlit and early shadows patterned the brickwork and were gathering in the niches and under the eaves. A blackbird flew out from under the apple tree near the front porch with its alarm signal echoing and fading as it fled.

Ralph gave a little shiver. 'Funny. No lights on. I wonder what Winifred's up to.'

Jules had caught the remark from his habit of watching the lips. 'Perhaps she's gone out Ralph.'

'We'll soon see.' Ralph strode to the door and let them both in.

The hall was in shadow. A coat hung on the bannister and a drip could be heard from the kitchen.

'Winifred, we're here. Where are you?' Ralph shouted.

He looked puzzled as he cocked his ear for any response. None came.

'I'm starting to get worried,' he said. 'You look in the front rooms Jules and I'll look in the back.'

No one was found.

'Hang on,' Ralph said. 'I'll try upstairs.'

He tore up the stairs and into their bedroom.

Winifred was lying sprawled across the bed. A basin rested by her head and Ralph could see blood in it. A blood-stained tea-towel lay at her side, one end dangling over the rim of the basin.

Ralph leapt forward and sat beside her. 'Winifred darling, what's happened?'

She stirred and gave a little moan. Her eyes opened slowly and she tried to focus.

'Hello,' she said but the words got caught up by the blood in her throat and came out as a vocalised gurgle. She tried to

180

struggle up.

'No, no. You stay down darling. You've had a nasty bleed. We must get the doctor.'

Winifred shook her head and managed a muffled 'no'.

'Oh yes, yes, yes' Ralph said sternly. 'Jules is just downstairs. I'll ask him to ring through.'

Dr Stewart had finished his evening surgery and was soon round. Within an hour an ambulance had taken Winifred to hospital.

That evening Ralph returned to an empty house. Jules had offered to keep him company but Ralph preferred to be alone.

He let himself in through the back door and noticed it gave squeaks he had not noticed before. He paused in the dark kitchen. The silence was oppressive. The house felt alien to him, indifferent, even a little hostile. How could it do this to me, Ralph thought? The house where we have been so happy. The spirit of the place seemed to him to have changed, but how can a place have a spirit, he thought? You're being silly Ralph me boy.

He switched on the kitchen light and it glared at him implacably. He wandered into the hall where he could almost hear the silence. His study would be friendly; he had spent countless happy hours in there and had sometimes dreaded people's footfall, even Winifred's, when he was immersed in his books or writing.

He opened the door. The armchair gaped at him, its cushions crumpled and today's paper folded over one of the arms. It did not seem to invite him. The sheets of his next sermon lay on the desk and the books in the shelves gazed out blankly. He had never felt that about them before. He slumped into the armchair and the paper slid with slow determination to the floor.

Upstairs felt just the same; silence and aloofness. He found it hard to believe this was the same friendly house where he and Winifred had lived happily all these years.

'Fickle place, he said aloud and the carpets and curtains absorbed his words as if he had not spoken them.

Just then the phone rang. 'Hello,' said Jules. 'How's Winifred?'

181

'She's quite comfortable. She's got a drip up but I'm not surprised at that. She looked ghastly didn't she? They think she's had a bleed from her stomach but it seems to have stopped so they're going to keep an eye on things for a while.'

'Thank goodness for that. Have you changed your mind about being on your own Ralph?'

'How did you guess, you crafty old devil? I would appreciate your company Jules, if you can come for a bit. This house seems a mite unfriendly. Seems to be missing Winifred. Can't think why. She's always messing it about, changing things around, scrubbing and polishing it. You'd think it would be glad of a rest, wouldn't you?'

'Well I'll be round right away and you can promise it that I won't be polishing or scrubbing it. How's that for a bargain?'

'Would you draw the line at peeling a few potatoes?'

Jules's presence seemed to brighten the house up a bit and Ralph felt nearer his normal contentment as they sat in his study after the meal.

He was seated in his own armchair and had brought in another easy chair for Jules, who sat where he could see Ralph's lip movements.

'It's funny how you get used to someone about the place,' Ralph said.

'And miss them when they're not there. I've never been in that position,' Jules went on. 'It's not quite the same with your parents, is it? After all, we've had to go away from them from time to time, most of us anyway, so we're used to it. I can't imagine what it must be like to have a wife.' He looked across at Ralph and grinned.

Ralph chuckled. 'If you're fishing for marital secrets and all that, I'm not obliging. But it is different. In a strange way it's as if you shared your life and yet, at the same time, you each have your own lives. Oh I don't know. It's difficult to explain.'

'I don't suppose I'll ever get married now,' Jules said pensively, with a sad shake of his head.

There was quite a long pause before Ralph spoke.

'The main impediment will be in you Jules. You will find that true, deep love has a way of ignoring "impediments" as you call them. As a matter of fact I should think we've all got some, but perhaps tucked away. However, they will come out and, if they were unexpected by the partner, can cause a deal of trouble. There's a lot to be said for impediments which are there, undisguisable, so that everyone knows where he or she is. In that case the initial hurdle is the worst, just making a start. It's your first hurdle you've got to worry about.'

'Yes, but I don't have to join the race, do I? I can go for a walk by myself.'

'And think how silly that is?'

Ralph could restrain himself no longer and leapt up from his chair, his eyes darting and his bony hands gesticulating.

'What on earth is life for if not to endeavour? What use is it washing at the end of the day if you've not got dirty? You lose the excitement of getting dirty and the pleasure of washing it off. Oh come on Jules, I know you better than that. That wouldn't do for you now, would it?'

'When you put it like that Ralph it seems irresistable but it doesn't always seem the same in the field.'

'Well of course that's where religion comes in. It is such a comfort to me Jules. I would be so happy to pass the faith on.' Ralph stared at Jules and smiled. 'Not yet, eh? Not ready yet? Please tell me when you are, won't you. In the meantime a cup of tea and to bed, don't you think?'

☆ ☆ ☆

Winifred had laser surgery to a bleeding point in her stomach and was soon home.

'The marvels of modern science,' Ralph said when she had sat down over tea. 'And I was just getting on top of things in the house.'

Winifred surveyed the stained traycloths, the ill-matched cups and the thick chunks of bread. She cast her eyes to the ceiling and spied a huge cobweb floating gracefully from the lights in the air currents.

'If you say so,' and she smiled sweetly. Ralph winked at her.

26

Fletcher had trained Sniffer to peak condition for smelling out drug smells and suddenly a bright idea came to him at breakfast.

'I've been thinking Doris.'

'Oh Lord! Not again. What is it this time?'

'Gilbert Blake has a video camera, hasn't he?'

'I really don't recall. I rather think he has though.'

'Well then, that's it.'

'Very clear. You're not contemplating a film career I hope?'

'No, but Sniffer is. Or rather I am for him.'

'What on earth do you mean?'

'I've got him finely tuned but nowhere to go. If I could demonstrate his prowess there might be a market for such pigs in HM Customs and Excise. I might become the first pig-drug-sniffer trainer, and purveyor,' he added.

'Sounds a mouthful.'

'I shall contact Gilbert at once.'

When approached on the subject Gilbert expressed interest until it dawned on him that Fletcher was contemplating the enterprise taking place in his, Gilbert's, own garden.

His enthusiasm nose-dived at that juncture and had to be revived by a strong dose of Fletcherian persuasion.

'Just think Gilbert, your garden would be the site of the very first recording of a new era of pig-drug-sniffers. You would get a mention in any self-respecting social history of England in this century, in any century for that matter. If it helped to lick the drug menace it would become a shrine. To the discriminating few,' he added hurriedly, envisaging queues of sightseers snaking out of Gilbert's drive into the road and hoping to subvert a similar picture in Gilbert's mind. 'Oh go on Gilbert. Be a sport.'

Gilbert yielded.

A date was arranged for the following Saturday. Later Fletcher saw Jules, Philip and Frank emerging from the church hall, following their practice session and a notion struck him.

'Jules,' he shouted across. Jules and the others paused.

'Hello Fletcher. How's life?'

'Fine. Excellent in fact. I've just thought up a rather good scheme.'

Jules pretended to make off at speed to the astonishment of the others.

'Where are you going Jules?' Philip asked.

'When Fletcher gets ideas one tends to head in another direction,' Jules shouted back.

'Oh come on Jules. That's hardly fair. Come back here. You haven't heard what's in my mind yet.'

'Ignorance is bliss,' Jules laughed, but he came back.

Gilbert explained his video venture. 'And it occurred to me,' he added, 'that a little music in the background would enhance things, give them a ring of authenticity.'

'Well, a ring of something,' Jules said. 'What do you say lads? Shall we do it. A musical accompaniment to a pig, a pig sniffing out drugs. Does that excite you?'

Philip and Frank grinned.

'Where would all this take place Fletcher? In your garden?'

Fletcher looked cunning and put his finger to the side of his nose. 'As a matter of fact Gilbert has volunteered to let us use his garden. It is larger and much more convenient.'

'You scheming devil,' Jules laughed. 'But what about a piano? I'm not carting mine out to Epping I can assure you.'

'I hadn't thought of that. That might pose a problem.'

'Possibly the first of many,' Jules said ominously. 'As a matter of fact, though I don't see why I should help you out, I do know where I can borrow an electric keyboard. It would be much more portable.'

186

Jules turned to Philip and Frank. 'We shall have to compose some suitable music then lads. You'd better start thinking about it. When's the big day Fletch?'

'Next Saturday. I wanted to catch Sniffer while he's in the peak of condition, and before poor old Gilbert starts to have second thoughts. I don't imagine Marigold will be too pleased.'

'We'll come up with something, won't we lads?'

They nodded assent.

Saturday dawned bright. Sniffer was loaded into the trailer with little protest and Fletcher and Doris took their places in the front.

An attempt to wedge the musical trio plus their instruments into the back seats had been witnessed and repudiated by Ralph, who insisted on taking them in his car, to the mixed feelings of Fletcher.

'That increases our chances of something going wrong, lets say twofold,' he observed to Doris.

'Perhaps tenfold?' They both laughed.

The expedition rolled up outside Gilbert's house in good order and was greeted by a large reception committee, Fiona having asked Boris and several other guests.

Gilbert whirred his video camera as they alighted and picked up Sniffer as he stumbled down the ramp with a squeal.

'That may be music to your ears,' Gilbert observed to Fletcher, 'but it's not quite what we were expecting.'

Just then Frank knocked his bass as he got out and it omitted a sonorous low note.

'There's no fog,' Marigold laughed.

Jules pretended to be angry. 'You just wait,' he said.

Sniffer was escorted into Gilbert's capacious back garden. Signs of defensive activity were manifest in the form of chestnut paling and other impediments which barricaded off the more precious of Gilbert's plants and equipment.

'I see you are prepared for anything,' Fletcher observed wryly.

Some packing cases and an old suitcase were positioned at the bottom of the garden where it abutted on to Epping Forest and Fletcher drew out his drug substitute.

'Ralph, could you put a pinch or two of this into one of the packing cases and place it in the middle of the pile while I attend to Sniffer here?'

The musicians set up their stance to the side nearer to the house so that the power cable would reach them.

The sheets of music they had prepared waved in the soft breeze and were eventually secured with Blu-tac.

'I have prepared a short commentary,' said Fletcher. 'Are you ready musicians? And you Gilbert?' All nodded.

Gentle music started and Fletcher began with Gilbert's video trained upon him.

'From the truffle-hunters of Perigord,' he held up a piece of trimmed mushroom, 'to the drug-sniffers of Epping Forest is a logical step which it has taken mankind some time to make. Who would have thought that the first step on the moon would precede it? But here we are at last on this significant day in 1993.'

At this stage Fletcher motioned for Doris to release Sniffer. She did so.

For a moment he stood as if undecided what to do. Then he made a sudden beeline for Ralph, who was standing to one side.

Ralph saw the pig's approach with some alarm and took evasive action across the lawn towards the forest side.

'That's extraordinary,' said Fletcher. Then, seeing Gilbert filming away gleefully, he added hastily, 'cut, Gilbert, cut.'

'Not on your nelly,' Gilbert said.

He swept the lens across the lawn to pick up Ralph and Sniffer. By now Sniffer had caught up with his quarry and was tearing at one of his pockets. In desperation Ralph plunged through the hedge and disappeared into the vastness of the forest, pursued by Sniffer.

Fletcher burst out laughing. 'I know what has happened.' Gilbert trained the camera back on him muttering. 'This I must not miss'.

188

'Ralph's gone and put the rest of the drug packet into his pocket and Sniffer's after that.'

Everyone roared with laughter. Then they paused to listen.

Sounds of crashing branches and piggish squeals of excitement came to their ears.

'I think Sniffer's found,' someone said and they all burst out laughing again.

'Do you think we ought to call him off?' Fletcher enquired of the company.

'I think it's about time,' Doris said. 'Poor old Ralph. He seems a bit prone to this sort of thing.'

An expedition party of Fletcher, Jules, Philip and Frank, trailed by the faithful Gilbert still filming, set off into the forest. It was not difficult to find their quarry.

'We don't need our noses here,' Fletcher said as sounds of squeals and protestation blended in the air.

They came upon Ralph half fallen across a broken branch, with Sniffer eagerly rifling his right-hand jacket pocket.

'Call him off for goodness sake,' Ralph pleaded. 'I'd forgotten the packet of drugs. I stuffed it into my pocket.'

'It's not easy to call off a determined pig,' Fletcher said pretending to be serious.

Then, feeling compassion for Ralph, he produced a well-sealed packet and opened it.

'Here we are. I brought this for just such a contingency. Well, almost this sort of contingency.'

Ralph readily consigned his packet to Fletcher who deftly stowed it away in his. Sniffer looked round as if to say 'what next'.

The party returned to base to applause from the spectators. Ralph was given a special cheer.

'We thought you must have got some aniseed on you,' Marigold said.

'No, I had some of the drug,' Ralph said ruefully.

'Do you think Sniffer is game for the real thing now?' Boris asked.

'You'd better make it snappy or I'll run out of film,' Gilbert said. 'I'd hate to miss anything. Might be a bit of an anticlimax

189

though after this lot.'

The music was restarted and Sniffer was once more released, this time with Ralph perched high on a wall.

All went according to plan and the filming ended with a flourish from the musicians, while Fletcher caressed Sniffer, who was looking up regretfully at Ralph.

Marigold served refreshments and the party broke up. When they reached home Ralph dropped off Philip and Frank and set off with Jules to return the keyboard.

'Would you say today was a successful day?' Jules asked, glancing wickedly at Ralph.

'Did you say stressful?' They both laughed.

'I've had a wonderful day,' Jules said. 'And so have Philip and Frank. They told me so. You're a great fellow Ralph, do you know that?'

'Just can't help it,' Ralph grinned at Jules. 'Just comes naturally.'

'Well, I hope you never change Ralph. You've done me a power of good, and young Philip. I came across a song of Benjamin Britten's the other day and I thought of you. He has set to music a poem by Pushkin. Do you want to hear it? I learnt it off.'

'Go ahead.'

Jules sang softly:

> 'At Eden's gate a gentle angel
> With lowered head stood shining bright,
> While Satan, sullen and rebellious
> O'er Hell's abysses took his flight.
> Soul of negation, soul of envy,
> He gazed at that angelic light,
> And warm and tender glowed within him
> A strange confusion at the sight.
> Forgive he said now I have seen thee,
> Not vainly did'st thou shine so bright;
> Not all in heaven have I hated,
> Not all things human earn my spite.'

190

Ralph was silent when Jules had finished.

At last he spoke. 'Have I done that to the Devil? Do you really think so Jules? That's the biggest compliment I've ever had. Poor old chap!'

'Who, me?'

'No. The Devil. You're all right.'

27

Jules found that the next few months flew swiftly and Peter and Mary were gratified to see it. His piano playing reached lyrical heights which won him acclaim in the British world of music, acclaim which Boris could not reach and, strangely he found, did not seek to reach. It was almost as if his success with Fiona rendered him competent but lacking the edge of his more anguished friend.

Each would go to such of the other's concerts as he could manage to attend and would often, after the performance, chat things over, both memories of the past and aspirations for the future.

More often than not Fiona would join them and Jules found he could now enjoy her friendship without trepidation, an attitude shared by Fiona and noted with approval by Boris.

'It's funny,' Boris observed on one such evening when the three of them were sitting in a café near the Wigmore Hall, 'how I seem content to be pedestrian. As long as I get enough contracts to fill my weeks I am satisfied, isn't that so Fiona?'

Fiona nodded. 'Yes dear. You keep a good steady pace, I'll say that.'

Boris turned to Jules. 'I can't reach your heights Jules. I sometimes wonder why. Well, I think I know why really.'

'I don't know about that Boris.' Jules smiled at him. 'You do very well, always. Sometimes I hit the deck.'

'Not often though, more often you're up there.' Boris waved his hand aloft and nearly knocked over a passing waiter's tray. 'Sorry,' he said as he turned round.

193

'I suppose I am conscious of a limited time for me. It adds a sort of zest to things once you accept it,' Jules said.

'Come on now Jules, what do you mean, limited time?' Fiona sounded quite indignant. 'Even if your deafness gets worse, you'll still be able to play, and do your teaching and so forth. Don't go back on all you've achieved, I've seen the results, we all have.'

'Yes, I agree,' Boris added.

Jules grinned at them. 'Things have gone quite well really, I must say. Could have been worse anyway. As a matter of fact I've started composing a bit, nothing much, not yet anyway, but it's a start I suppose.'

'That's wonderful,' Fiona said.

'Is it advanced stuff?' Boris asked. 'Probably I shouldn't even be able to play it.'

'Oh, come now Boris, don't underrate yourself.'

A thought struck Boris, he whispered to Fiona and she nodded.

'Hey, what's all the secrecy all of a sudden? Out with it now.' Jules cupped his ears and watched Boris's face.

'We were wondering whether you would compose and play something for our wedding? How about it Jules?'

'I know it might be asking rather a lot one way or the other,' Fiona added, looking earnestly at Jules, 'but would you?'

'Of course I would. For my two best pals; with all my heart.'

At the wedding Jules played a piano piece which plumbed the depths of sorrow and reached the heights of passion. All who heard it were moved.